The colossal spider was upon him. Reflections from Conan's torch danced in the creature's four great round eyes.

Below these eyes, a pair of hairy, jointed append- ages extended forward like arms. As these organs reached out for Conan, he smote one of them with his hammer.

Then the monster advanced again. Conan felt like a fly caught in a web, awaiting its fate. The spider's fangs now spread horizontally to pierce Conan's body from opposite sides; green venom dripped from their hollow points. Between and below the fangs, the jointed mouth parts worked hungrily.

For a heartbeat the pair confronted each other, Conan with his hammer raised to deliver one last crushing blow before he died...

Chronological order of the CONAN series:

CONAN
CONAN OF CIMMERIA
CONAN THE FREEBOOTER
CONAN THE WANDERER
CONAN THE ADVENTURER
CONAN THE BUCCANEER
CONAN THE WARRIOR
CONAN THE USURPER
CONAN THE CONQUEROR
CONAN THE AVENGER
CONAN OF AQUILONIA
CONAN OF THE ISLES
CONAN THE SWORDSMAN
CONAN THE LIBERATOR
CONAN THE SWORD OF SKELOS
CONAN THE ROAD OF KINGS
CONAN THE REBEL
CONAN AND THE SPIDER GOD

Illustrated CONAN novels:

CONAN AND THE SORCERER
CONAN: THE FLAME KNIFE
CONAN THE MERCENARY
THE TREASURE OF TRANICOS

Other CONAN novels:

THE BLADE OF CONAN
THE SPELL OF CONAN

CONAN
AND THE
SPIDER GOD

L. Sprague de Camp

ACE BOOKS, NEW YORK

This Ace book contains the complete
text of the original edition.
It has been completely reset in a typeface
designed for easy reading, and was printed
from new film.

CONAN AND THE SPIDER GOD

An Ace Book / published by arrangement with
Conan Properties, Inc.

PRINTING HISTORY
Bantam Books edition / December 1980
Ace edition / April 1989

ISBN: 0-441-11609-4

Ace Books are published by The Berkley Publishing Group,
200 Madison Avenue, New York, NY 10016.
The name "ACE" and the "A" logo
are trademarks belonging to Charter Communications, Inc.
PRINTED IN THE UNITED STATES OF AMERICA

10 9 8 7 6 5 4 3 2 1

Contents

	INTRODUCTION	vii
I.	LUST AND DEATH	1
II.	THE SWAMP CAT	10
III.	THE BLIND SEER	19
IV.	THE GOLDEN DRAGON	29
V.	THE CITY ON THE CRAG	45
VI.	THE TEMPLE OF THE SPIDER	56
VII.	WINE OF KYROS	70
VIII.	THE EIGHT EYES OF ZATH	87
IX.	THE POWDER OF FORGETFULNESS	96
X.	THE TIGER'S FANG	105
XI.	THE STENCH OF CARRION	116
XII.	THE CHILDREN OF ZATH	134

Introduction

Conan, the magnificent barbarian adventurer, grew up in the mind of Robert Ervin Howard, the Texan pulp writer, in 1932. As Howard put it, the character "grew up in my mind . . . when I was stopping in a little border town on the lower Rio Grande . . . . He simply stalked full grown out of oblivion and set me to work recording the saga of his adventures. . . . Some mechanism in my sub-consciousness took the dominant characteristics of various prize-fighters, gunmen, bootleggers, oil field bullies, gamblers, and honest workmen I have come in contact with, and combining them all, produced the amalgamation I call Conan the Cimmerian."

This is undoubtedly true. Yet, at the same time, Conan is an obvious idealization of Howard himself—Howard as he wished he were: a hell-raising, irresponsible adventurer, devoted to wine, women, and strife. For all his burly build—he was five feet eleven inches tall and weighed nearly two hundred pounds, most of it muscle—Robert Howard and the great Cimmerian were as different as day and night.

While both Howard and his hero had hot tempers and a chivalrous attitude towards women, Conan is portrayed as a pure extrovert, a roughneck with few inhibitions and a rudimentary conscience. His creator, on the other hand, was a morally upright man, meticulously law-abiding; courteous and tenderhearted; shy, bookish, introverted, and—although he denied it—a genuine intellectual. A moody man, he alternated between periods of cheerful, spellbind-

ing garrulity and spells of depression and despair. At the age
of thirty, with a promising literary career opening out before
him, he took his own life on the occasion of his aged
mother's death.

Born in Peaster, Texas, in 1906, Robert E. Howard spent
his adult years in the small town of Cross Plains, Texas, in
the center of the state. A shy and lonely child, he became a
voracious bookworm and a body-builder who enhanced his
naturally powerful physique by boxing, weight-lifting, and
riding. Among his favorite authors were Edgar Rice Bur-
roughs, Rudyard Kipling, Harold Lamb, Jack London, and
Talbot Mundy. With these interests, it is not surprising that
he wrote boxing stories, Western stories, tales of oriental
adventure, and a goodly volume of memorable verse.

Transcending all these, both in volume and in popularity,
were his fantasy stories. It was Howard's misfortune that
during the brief decade of his productive literary life, fantasy was held in low esteem. He did not live to see any of his
works appear in book form. Most of his imaginative tales
were published in *Weird Tales,* a magazine that led a precari-
ous existence from 1923 to 1954. Although its rates were
low and payments often late, Howard found it his most reli-
able market.

In the late 1920s, Howard wrote a series of fantasies
about King Kull, a native of lost Atlantis who becomes the
ruler of a mainland kingdom. The series had only limited
success; of the ten Kull stories he completed, Howard sold
three.

Later he rewrote an unsold Kull story, "By This Axe I
Rule!" The new tale, "The Phoenix on the Sword," was set
in a later imaginary period, Howard's Hyborian Age, a time
between the sinking of Atlantis and the beginnings of
recorded history. Howard gave his new hero the old Celtic
name of Conan; for, being of partly Irish ancestry himself,
Howard harbored an intense interest in and admiration for
the Celts.

"The Phoenix on the Sword" became a smash hit with the
readers of *Weird Tales.* Hence, from 1932 to 1936, most of
Howard's writing time was devoted to Conan stories,
although shortly before his death, he spoke of giving up fan-

tasy to concentrate on Westerns.

Of Howard's several heroes, Conan proved the most popular. Howard saw the publication of eighteen stories about the gigantic barbarian, who wades through rivers of gore to overthrow foes both natural and supernatural, and who at last becomes the ruler of the mightiest Hyborian kingdom.

Since Howard's death, several unpublished Conan stories, from complete manuscripts to mere fragments and synopses, have come to light through the efforts of Glenn Lord and myself. My colleague, Lin Carter, and I have completed the unfinished tales, and Carter and Björn Nyberg have collaborated with me on new Conan stories to fill the gaps in the saga.

In addition, several other colleagues—Karl Edward Wagner, Andrew Offutt, and Poul Anderson—have also tried their hands at Conan pastiches, a venerable form of literature in which a living author tries to recapture both the spirit and the style of a predecessor, as Virgil in his *Aeneid* did with Homer's epics. *Conan and the Spider God* is such a novel. To what extent any of us can recreate the vividness of Howard's narratives and the excellence of his style, the reader must judge for himself.

The Conan stories belong to a sub-genre of fantasy called heroic fantasy, or swordplay-and-sorcery fiction. This art form was originated in the 1880s by William Morris, the British artist, poet, decorator, manufacturer, and reformer, as a modern imitation of the medieval romance, which had been moribund since Cervantes burlesqued it with his *Don Quixote*. Morris was followed in the United Kingdom in the early twentieth century by Lord Dunsany and Eric Rücker Eddison, and in the United States by Robert Howard, Clark Ashton Smith, and many others.

Heroic fantasies are laid in an imaginary world—either long ago, or far into the future, or on another planet—where magic works, supernatural beings abound, and machinery does not exist. An adult fairy tale of this kind provides pure escape fiction. In such a world, gleaming cities raise their silver spires against the stars; sorcerers cast sinister spells from subterranean lairs; baleful spirits stalk crumbling ruins of immemorial antiquity; primeval monsters crash through jungle thickets; and the fate of kingdoms is balanced on the blades of broadswords brandished by heroes of preternatural strength and valor. Men are mighty, women are beautiful, problems are simple, life is adventurous, and nobody has ever heard of inflation, the petroleum shortage, or atmospheric pollution.

In other words, heroic fantasy sings of a world not as it is, but as it ought to be. Its aim is to entertain, not to display the author's cleverness, nor to uplift the reader, nor to expose the shortcomings of the world we live in. On the subject of pure escapism, J.R.R. Tolkien once remarked, "Why should a man be scorned if, finding himself in prison . . . he thinks and talks about other topics than jailers and prison-walls?"

During the Second World War, it appeared that fantasy had become a casualty of the machine age. Then, with the publication in the 1950s of Tolkien's three-volume novel *The Lord of the Rings,* and its later reprinting in paperback as a runaway best seller, the future of modern fantasy was assured.

In the 1960s, I managed to interest a paperback publisher in the whole series of the Conan stories, so that for the first time Howard's remarkable tales reached a mass audience. The resulting twelve volumes proved second only to *The Lord of the Rings* in popularity among works of fantasy, for here is a hero who bestrides the world, untrammeled by petty laws and hindrances; here is a tale told in vigorous, colorful style; here is man triumphant over soul-searing trials and tribulations. Here is the stuff that dreams are made of.

In the saga, Conan, the son of a blacksmith, is born in the bleak, barbarous northern land of Cimmeria. Forced by a feud to flee his tribe, he travels north to the sub-arctic land of Asgard, where he joins the Æsir in battles with the Vanir of Vanaheim to the west and the Hyperboreans to the east. In one of these forays he is captured and enslaved by the Hyperboreans. He escapes and makes his way south to the ancient land of Zamora. Lawless and green to the ways of civilization, Conan occupies himself for a couple of years as a thief, more daring than adroit, not only in Zamora but also in the neighboring realms of Corinthia and Nemedia.

Disgusted with this starveling, outcast existence, Conan treks eastward and enlists in the army of the mighty oriental kingdom of Turan, then ruled by the good-natured but ineffectual King Yildiz. Here he serves as a soldier for about two years, learning archery and horsemanship and traveling widely, once as far east as fabled Khitai.

As the present story opens, Conan, still in his early twenties, has risen to the rank of captain and has obtained a long-coveted transfer to the Royal Guard in the capital city of Aghrapur. As usual, trouble is his bedfellow; and circumstances soon compel him to seek his fortune elsewhere.

L. SPRAGUE DE CAMP
Villanova, Pennsylvania

I. Lust and Death

A tall, immensely powerful man—almost a giant—stood motionless in the shadows of the courtyard. Although he could see the candle that the Turanian woman had placed in the window as a sign that the coast was clear, and to a hill-man the climb was child's play, he waited. He had no desire to be caught halfway up the wall, clinging like a beetle to the ivy that mantled the ancient edifice. While the civic guard would hesitate to arrest one of King Yildiz's officers, word of his escapade would surely reach the ears of Narkia's protector. And this protector was Senior Captain Orkhan, the large man's commanding officer.

With alert blue eyes, Conan of Cimmeria, a captain in the Royal Guard, scanned the sky above, where the full moon dusted the domes and towers of Aghrapur with powdered silver. A cloud was bearing down upon the luminary; but this wind-borne galleon of the sky was inadequate for the Cimmerian's purpose. It would dim the moonlight for only half the time required to clamber up the ivy. A much larger cloud, he observed with satisfaction, sailed in the wake of the first.

When the moon had veiled her face behind the more voluminous cloud, Conan hitched his baldric around so that the sword hung down between his shoulders. He slipped off his sandals and tucked them into his belt; then, grasping the

1

heavy, knotted vines with fingers and toes, he mounted with catlike agility.

Across the shadowed spires and roofs lay a ghostly silence, broken but rarely by the sound of hurrying feet; while overhead the cloud, outlined in vermeil, billowed slowly past. The climber felt a thin wind stir his square-cut black mane, and a tiny shiver shook him. He remembered the words of the astrologer whom he had consulted three days before.

"Beware of launching an enterprise at the next full of the moon," the graybeard had said. "The stellar aspects imply that you would thus set in motion wheels within wheels of cause and effect—a vast concatenation of dire changes."

"Will the result be good or bad?" demanded Conan.

The astrologer shrugged the bony shoulders under his patched robe. "That cannot be foreseen; save that it would be something drastic. There would ensue great overturns."

"Can't you even tell whether I shall end up on the top of the heap or at the bottom?"

"Nay, Captain. Since I see in the stars no great benison for you, meseems the bottom were more likely."

Grumbling at this uninspiring prediction, Conan paid up and departed. He did not disbelieve in any form of magic, sorcery, or spiritism; but he had an equal faith in the fallibility of individual occultists. Their ranks, he thought, were at least as full of fakers and blunderers as any other occupation. So, when Narkia had sent him a note inviting him to call while her protector was away, he had not let the astrologer's warning stop him.

The candle vanished, and the window creaked open. The giant eeled through and slid to his feet. He stared hungrily at the Turanian woman who stood before him. Her black hair cascaded down her supple shoulders, while the glow of the candle, now resting on the taboret beside her, revealed her splendid body through her diaphanous gown of amethyst silk.

"Well, here I am," rumbled Conan.

Narkia's feline eyes sparkled with amusement as they rested on the man who towered over her in a cheap woolen tunic and patched, baggy pantaloons.

"I have awaited your coming, Conan," she replied, moving forward with welcoming arms outstretched. "Though, in sooth, I did not expect to find you looking like a stable hand. Where are your splendid cream-and-scarlet uniform and silver-spurred boots?"

"I didn't think it sensible to wear them tonight," he said abruptly, lifting his baldric over his head and laying his sword carelessly on the carpet. Beneath his square-cut black mane, deep set blue eyes under heavy black brows burned in a scarred and swarthy face. Although he was only in his early twenties, the vicissitudes of a wild, hard life had stamped him with the harsh appearance of maturity.

With the lithe motion of a tiger, Conan glided forward, gathered the wench into his brawny arms, and wheeled her toward the bed. But Narkia resisted, pushing her palms against his massive chest.

"Stay!" she breathed. "You barbarians are too impulsive. First, we needs must cultivate our acquaintance. Sit on yonder stool and have a sip of wine!"

"If I must," grumbled Conan, speaking Hyrkanian with a barbarous accent. Unwillingly he sat and, in three gulps, drained the proffered goblet of golden fluid.

"My thanks, girl," he muttered, setting the empty vessel down on the little table.

Narkia clucked. "Really, Captain Conan, you are a boor! A fine vintage from Iranistan should be sipped and savored slowly, but you pour it down like bitter beer. Will you never become civilized?"

"I doubt it," grunted Conan. "What I have seen of your so-called civilization in the last few years has not filled me with any great love of it."

"Then why stay here in Turan? You could return to your barbarous homeland—wherever that be."

With a wry grin, Conan clasped his massive hands behind his shaggy head and leaned back against the tapestried wall. "Why do I stay?" he shrugged. "I suppose because there is more gold to be gathered here, one way or another; also more things to see and do. Life in a Cimmerian village grows dull after a while—the same old round, day after day, save for petty quarrels with the other villagers and now and then a feud with a neighboring clan. Now, here—what's that?"

Booted feet tramped upon the stair, and in an instant the door burst open. In the black opening stood Senior Captain Orkhan, jaw sagging with astonishment beneath his spired, turban-wound helmet. Orkhan was a tall, hawk-featured man, less massive than Conan but strong and lithe, although the first gray hairs had begun to sprout in his close-cut dark beard.

As he studied the tableau, and recognition replaced astonishment, Orkhan's face reddened with rising wrath. "So!" he grated. "When the cat's away . . ." His hand went to the hilt of his scimitar.

The instant the door swung open, Narkia had thrown herself back on the bed. As Orkhan spoke, she cried: "Rape! This savage burst in, threatening to kill—"

In confusion, Conan glanced from one to the other before his brain, caught up in the whirl of events, grew clear. As Orkhan's sword sang from its sheath, the Cimmerian sprang to his feet, snatched up the stool on which he had been sitting, and hurled it at his assailant. The missile struck the Turanian in the belly, sending him staggering back. Meanwhile, Conan dove for his own sword, lying in its scabbard on the floor. By the time Orkhan had recovered, Conan was up and armed.

"Thank Erlik you've come, my lord!" gasped Narkia, huddling back on the bed. "He would have—"

As she spoke, Conan met a whirlwind attack by Orkhan, who bored in, striking forehand, backhand, and overhand in rapid succession. Conan grimly parried each vicious cut. The blades clashed, clanged, and ground together, striking sparks. The swordplay was all cut-and-parry, since the curved Turanian saber was ill-adapted to thrusting.

"Stop it, you fool!" roared Conan. "The woman lies! I came at her invitation, and we have done naught—"

Narkia screamed something that Conan failed to comprehend; for, as Orkhan pressed his attack, red battle rage surged up in Conan's veins. He struck harder and faster, until Orkhan, skilled swordsman though he was, fell back breathing heavily.

Then Conan's sword, flashing past Orkhan's guard, sheared through the links of the Turanian's mesh-mail vest and sliced into his side. Orkhan staggered, dropping his weapon and pressing a hand against his wound, while blood seeped out between his fingers. Conan followed the first telling blow with a slash that bit deeply into Orkhan's neck. The Turanian fell heavily, shuddered, and lay still, while dark stains spread across the carpet on which he sprawled.

"You've slain him!" shrieked Narkia. "Tughril will have your head for that. Why could you not have stunned him with the flat?"

"When you're fighting for your life," grunted Conan, wiping and sheathing his blade, "You cannot measure out your strokes with the nicety of an apothecary compounding a potion. It's as much your fault as mine. Why did you accuse me of rape, girl?"

Narkia shrugged. With a trace of a mischievous smile, she said: "Because I knew not which of you would win; and had I not accused you, and he slew you, he'd have killed me for good measure."

"That's civilization for you!" sneered Conan. Before lifting his baldric to slide it over his head, he whirled and slapped Narkia on the haunch with the scabbarded blade, bowling her over in an untidy heap. She shrank back, eyes big with fear.

"If you were not a woman," he growled, "it would go hard with you. I warn you to give me an hour ere you cry the alarm. If you do not . . ." Scowling, he drew a finger across his throat and backed to the window. An instant later he was swarming down the ivy, while Narkia's curses floated after him on the moonlit air.

Lyco of Khorshemish, lieutenant in the King's Light Horse, was playing a plaintive air on his flute when Conan burst into the room they shared on Maypur Alley. Muttering a hasty greeting, Conan hurriedly changed from civilian garb into his officer's uniform. Then he spread his blanket on the floor and began placing his meager possessions upon it. He opened a locked chest and drew out a small bag of coin.

"Whither away?" asked Lyco, a stocky, dark man of about Conan's age. "One would think you were leaving for good. Is some fiend after you?"

"I am and it is," grunted Conan.

"What have you been up to? Raiding the King's harem? Why in the name of the gods, when you have at last attained the easy duty you've been angling for?"

Conan hesitated, then said: "You might as well know, since I shall be hence ere you could betray me."

Lyco started a hot protest, but Conan waved him to silence. "I did but jest, Lyco. I've just killed Orkhan." Tersely, he gave an account of the evening's events.

Lyco whistled. "That spills the stew-pot into the fire! The High Priest of Erlik is his sire. Old Tughril will have your heart's blood, even if you could win the King's forgiveness."

"I know it," gritted Conan, tying up his blanket roll. "That's why I'm in a hurry."

"Had you also slain the woman, you could have made it seem an ordinary robbery, with nobody the wiser."

"Trust a Kothian to think of that!" snarled Conan. "I'm not yet civilized enough to kill women out of hand. If I stay long enough in these southlands, I may yet learn."

"Well, trust a thick-headed Cimmerian to blunder into traps, one after another! I told you the omens were unfavorable tonight, and that my dream of last night boded ill."

"Aye; you dreamed some foolishness that had naught to do with me—about a wizard seizing a priceless gem. You should have been a seer rather than a soldier, my lad."

Lyco rose. "Do you need more coin?"

Conan shook his head. "That is good of you; but I have enough to get me to some other kingdom. Thank Erlik, I've saved a little from my pay. If you pull the right strings, Lyco, you might get promoted to my post."

"I might; but I'd rather have my old comrade-in-arms about to trade insults with. What shall I tell people?"

Conan paused, frowning. "Crom, what a complicated business! Tell them I came in with some cock-and-bull story of a royal message to be carried to—to—what's that little border kingdom southeast of Koth?"

"Khauran?"

"Aye, a message to the King of Khauran."

"They have a queen there."

"The queen, then. Farewell, and in a fight never forget to guard your crotch!"

They made their adieus in bluff, soldierly fashion, wringing hands, slapping backs, and punching each other's shoulders. Then Conan was gone, in a swirl of saffron cloak.

The rotund moon, declining in the western sky, gazed placidly down upon the West Gate of Aghrapur as Conan trotted up on his big black destrier, Egil. His belongings in the blanket roll were lashed securely to his saddle, behind the cantle.

"Open up!" he called. "I'm Captain Conan of the King's Royal Guard, on a royal commission!"

"What is your mission, Captain?" demanded the officer of the gate guard.

Conan held up a roll of parchment. "A message from His Majesty to the Queen of Khauran. I must deliver it forthwith."

While grunting soldiers pulled on the bronze-studded oaken portal, Conan tucked the parchment into the wallet that hung from his belt. The scroll was in reality a short treatise on swordsmanship, on which Conan had been practicing his limited knowledge of written Hyrkanian, and he had counted upon the guards' not bothering to inspect it. Even if they had, he felt sure that few, if any, of them could read the document, especially by lantern light.

At last the gate creaked open. With a wave, Conan trotted through and broke into a canter. He followed the broad highway, which some in these parts called the Road of Kings—one of several thoroughfares so named—leading westward to Zamora and the Hyborian kingdoms. He rode steadily through the dying night, past fields of young spring wheat, past luxuriant pastures where shepherds watched their flocks and neatherds tended their cattle.

Before the road reached Shadizar, the capital of Zamora, a path led up into the hills bordering Khauran. Conan, however, had no intention of going to Khauran. As soon as he was out of sight of Aghrapur, he pulled off the road at a place where scrubby trees bordered a watercourse. Out of sight of passersby he dismounted, tethered his horse, stripped off his handsome uniform, and donned the shabby civilian tunic and trews in which he had made his ill-fated visit to Narkia.

As Conan changed clothes, he cursed himself for an addlepated fool. Lyco was right; he was a fool. The woman had slipped him a note, inviting him to her apartment while her protector was away in Shahpur; and, tired of tavern wenches, Conan aspired to a courtesan of higher rank and quality. For this, and for the boyish thrill of stealing his commander's girl out from under that officer's nose, he had cut short a promising career. He had never imagined that Orkhan might return from Shahpur earlier than expected. The worst of it was that he had never disliked the fellow; a strict officer but a fair one. . . .

Sunk in melancholy gloom, Conan unwound the turban from his spired helmet and draped the cloth over his head in imitation of a Zuagir kaffiyya, tucking the ends inside his tunic. Then he repacked his belongings, mounted, and set out briskly—but not back to the Road of Kings. Instead, he headed north across country, over fields and through woods where none could track his horse's hoofprints.

He smiled grimly when, far behind, he heard the drumming of hooves as a body of horsemen raced westward along the main road. Traveling in that direction, they would never catch him.

Half an hour later, in the violet dawn, Conan was walking his horse northward along a minor road that was little more than a track through a region of scrubby second growth. So full was his head of alternative plans and routes that for an instant he failed to mark the sound of hooves, the creak of harness, and the jingle of accouterments of approaching horsemen. Before he had time to turn his horse into the concealing scrub, the riders galloped around a bend in the track and rode straight for him. They were a squad of King Yildiz's horse archers on foam-flecked mounts.

Cursing his inattention, Conan pulled off to the roadside, uncertain whether to fight or flee. But the soldiers clattered past with scarcely a glance in his direction. The last man in the column, an officer, pulled up long enough to shout:

"You there, fellow! Have you seen a party of travelers with a woman?"

"Why—" Conan started an angry retort before he remembered that he was no longer Captain Conan of the King's Royal Guard. "Nay, sir, I have not," he growled, with an unconvincing show of humility.

Cursing by his gods, the officer spurred his horse after the rest of the squad. For Conan, as he resumed his northward trot, astonishment trod on the heels of relief. Something must have happened in Aghrapur—something of more moment than his affair with Orkhan. The squad that had rushed past had not even been interested in ascertaining his identity. Could it be that the force pounding westward along the Road of Kings also pursued some quarry other than the renegade Captain Conan?

Perhaps he would unravel the tangle in Sultanapur.

II. The Swamp Cat

Traveling through the Marshes of Mehar proved no less oner-
ous than guiding a camel across a featureless desert or con-
ning a boat on the boundless sea. On all sides reeds, taller
than Conan's horse, stretched away to infinity. The yellowed
canes of last year's crop rattled monotonously whenever a
breeze rippled across them; while below, the tender green
shoots of the new growth crowded the earth and provided
Egil with fodder.

A rider through the marshes was forced to set his course
by sun and stars. A man afoot would find this task all but
impossible, for the towering reeds would obscure all view
saved that of the sky directly overhead.

From the back of his stallion, Conan could look out across
the tops of the reeds, which undulated gently like the waves
of a placid sea. When he reached one of the rare rises of
ground, he sometimes glimpsed the Vilayet Sea afar to his
right. On his left he often sighted the tops of the low hills
that sundered the Marshes of Mehar from the Turanian
steppe.

Conan had swum his horse across the Ilbars River below
Akif and headed north, keeping the sea in view. He reasoned
that, to escape his pursuers' notice, he must either lose himself in an urban crowd or seek the solitude of some uninhab-
ited place, whence he could be forewarned of his pursuers if
they picked up his trail.

Conan had never before seen the Marshes of Mehar. Rumor reported them as solitary a lieu as any place on earth. The waterlogged soil was useless for farming. Timber was limited to a few dwarfish, twisted trees, crowning occasional knobby knolls. Biting insects were alleged to swarm in such numbers that even hunters, who might otherwise have invaded the marshes in pursuit of wild swine and other game, forswore to seek their prey there.

The marshes, moreover, were said to be the abode of a dangerous predator, vaguely referred to as the "swamp cat." Although Conan had never met anyone who claimed to have seen such a creature, all agreed that it was as deadly as a tiger.

Still, the dismal solitude of the marshes exceeded Conan's expectations. Here no sound broke the silence save the plashing of Egil's muddy hooves, the rustling of the reeds, and the buzz and hum of clouds of insects, which swirled up from the agitated canes. With his turban cloth securely wrapped around his head and face and his uniform gauntlets on his hands, Conan was well protected; but his miserable mount kept lashing his tail and shaking his mane to dislodge the myriad pests.

For days on end, Conan plodded through the changeless reeds. Once he started a sounder of swine of a large, rust-red species. Avid for some fresh pork to vary his dwindling supply of salted meat and hard biscuits, he reached for his bow; but by the time he had pulled the short, double-curved Hyrkanian weapon from its case, the pigs had vanished. Conan decided against the unwelcome delay of an extended hunt.

For three days Conan forged ahead, while the reeds before him still stretched to the horizon. Toward the close of the third day, when a hillock afforded a vista, he found that both the sea on his right and the hills on the western horizon had moved closer than before. Guessing that he was nearing the northern end of the marshes and, beyond that, the city of Sultanapur, he clucked Egil to a trot.

Then, thin in the distance, he heard a human cry; he thought he detected several voices shouting. Turning his head, he located the source of the commotion on a hillock to his left, whence a plume of blue smoke ascended lazily into the sky. Prudence told Conan to ride on, regardless of the cause of the disturbance. The fewer who saw him while he was still in Turan, the better were his chances of escaping that kingdom unscathed.

But prudence had never occupied the first rank among Conan's counselors; and a camp implied a fresh-cooked meal, and, beyond that, the possibility of loot or legitimate employment. Besides, his curiosity was aroused. While Conan was capable of ruthless action in pursuit of his own interests, he could also, on a quixotic impulse, throw himself into some affair that was none of his business when his barbaric notions of honor required it.

On this occasion, curiosity and thoughts of food vanquished caution. Conan turned Egil's head toward the hillock and heeled the horse into a fast trot. As he approached, he described some agitated figures rushing about on the crest of the knoll, among clumps of spring wildflowers whose scarlet, golden, and violet blooms lent a rare touch of color to the drab landscape.

As he came closer, he perceived that there were five men, moving around a small tent adjacent to their campfire. Their beasts of burden—four asses, two horses, and a camel—had been securely tethered to a gnarled, dwarfish tree; now terrified, they were bucking and straining at their tethers despite the efforts of one of the men to calm them.

"What's the matter?" Conan roared across the rustle of the reeds.

"Beware! Swamp cat!" shouted one of the men, a lean fellow in a white turban.

"Where?" yelled Conan.

The men around the tent babbled all at once, pointing in various directions. Then a spitting snarl ripped the air on Conan's right, and out of the reeds bounded a tawny creature whose like Conan had never beheld. The head and forequarters were those of a large member of the cat tribe, but the hindlegs were twice as long as those of a normal feline. The beast progressed by gigantic leaps, its heavy tail held stiffly out behind for balance, presenting to view a bazarre combination of a panther and a gigantic hare.

Sighting the approaching menace, the stallion whinnied in fear and leaped convulsively to one side. During his two years of service with the Turanian army, Conan had become an accomplished rider; but he still lacked the consummate skill of a Hyrkanian nomad, reared in the saddle. Caught by surprise, Conan pitched headlong off his mount, landing heavily on his shoulder in a mass of reeds. With a thunder of hooves, Egil vanished.

In a flash, Conan rolled to his feet and whipped out his scimitar. The swamp cat had alighted within a spear's length of the Cimmerian, with its fur erect and its eyes ablaze. Bracing himself for the attack, Conan raised his weapon and uttered the fearsome battle cry of the Cimmerian tribes.

At that dreadful, inhuman scream, the cat paused, snarling. Then it leaped—but not at Conan. The beast sprang away at an angle and began to circle the knoll. On the crest of the low eminence, the five travelers rushed to intercept it, armed with spears, daggers, and a solitary sword. But the swamp cat was more interested in the travelers' tethered animals than in human prey.

Conan dashed up the slope to the top of the rise, where the campfire crackled cheerfully. Seizing a blazing faggot, he sped on, heading straight for the swamp cat, which crouched in preparation for another of its gargantuan leaps. Conan's quick movement caused the log to blaze up, and he thrust the blazing end into the cat's face.

With a shriek, the creature sprang back, turned, and bounded mewling away into the reeds, leaving a faint trail of smoke from its singed hair and whiskers.

As Conan walked back up the slope, the traveler with the sword and turban stepped forward to greet him. This man, a slender fellow of early middle age, with a pointed black beard, seemed better accoutered than the others and somewhat taller, although all five were small, dark, and slender—mere pygmies compared to the giant Cimmerian.

"We are grateful, sir," the turbaned man began. "The beast would have borne off one or more of our mounts, leaving us stranded in this devil-haunted wilderness."

Conan nodded curtly. "It's naught. Who will help me to catch my nag, if the swamp cat hasn't eaten him?"

"Take my horse, sir," said the leader. "Dinak, saddle the baggage horse and accompany our visitor."

As the tethered animal was still skittish from its confrontation with the swamp cat, Conan had much ado to calm it. Eventually he swung into the saddle and set out after Egil, with Dinak trotting behind him. The trail through the trampled reeds was not hard to follow, and Conan turned in the saddle to say:

"You're Zamorians, are you not?"

"Aye, sir."

"I thought I knew that accent. Who is your leader, the man with the turban?"

"He is called Harpagus. We are merchants. And you, sir?"

"Merely an out-of-work mercenary."

It was on the tip of Conan's tongue to ask Dinak why the Zamorians were taking an unmarked route through this inhospitable wilderness instead of following the highway that paralleled their course beyond the westward hills. But when it occurred to him that the Zamorian might well ask the same question of him, Conan held his peace and bent his attention to the trail.

As the red ball of the sun hung above the dark line of the western hills, they caught up with Conan's horse nibbling on reed sprouts. Before night had swallowed the twilight, Conan had led the truant Egil back to the encampment. One of the Zamorians was roasting a leg of lamb for dinner, and Conan's nostrils quivered at the scent. He and Dinak unsaddled their mounts and tethered them within easy reach of the clumps of flower-bearing herbs that dotted the hillock.

"Join us, I pray you," invited Harpagus.

"Gladly," said Conan. "I haven't tasted a cooked repast since entering this forsaken marsh. Who lies within?" He jerked a thumb toward the tent, whence a slender hand was reaching out to take a plate of provender.

Harpagus paused before answering. "A lady," he said at last, "who does not wish to be seen by strangers."

Conan shrugged and addressed himself to his food. He could have eaten twice the portions that the Zamorians had served him, but he stretched his meager meal with a couple of stale biscuits from his saddle bags.

One Zamorian produced a skin of wine, which the men passed around, taking gulps from the muzzle. Combing his beard with his fingers, one of which bore a huge, ornate ring, Harpagus said:

"If I may make so bold, young sir, who are you and how came you upon us so opportunely?"

Conan shrugged. "Mere happenstance. As I told Dinak here, I am only a wandering soldier."

"Then you should be traveling toward Aghrapur instead of away from it. That is where you will find the recruiting officers for King Yildiz's army."

"I have other plans," said Conan shortly, wishing he were quick-witted enough to think up plausible lies. Then, suddenly, Harpagus turned, alerted by the soft crunch of a foot on the dried stems of last year's vegetation. Following the Zamorian's glance, Conan saw that a slender female figure had emerged from the obscurity of the tent.

Illumined by the flickering firelight, the woman appeared to be a decade older than Conan, comely of person, and richly clad in garments more suitable for a lordly Hyrkanian's harem than for travel in the wilderness. The firelight was reflected in the links of a golden chain about her columnar neck; and from the chain hung an enormous gem, of purplish hue, in an ornate setting. While the light was too weak for Conan to pick out details, such an ornament, he knew, bespoke the wealth of princes. As the woman slowly approached the fire, Conan perceived her curiously blank stare, like that of a sleep-walker.

"Ja—my lady!" Harpagus' voice rose sharply. "You were bidden to remain within the tent."

"It's cold," murmured the woman. "Cold in the tent." She stretched pale hands toward the flames, glancing unseeingly at Conan and away again into the night.

Harpagus rose, grasped the woman's shoulders, and turned her around. "Look!" he said. Before the woman's face he waved a hand that bore a ring with a great fiery gemstone, muttering: "You shall reënter the tent. You shall speak to no one. You shall forget all that you have seen. You shall reënter the tent. . . ."

After several repetitions, the woman bowed her head and silently retraced her steps, dropping the tent flap behind her. Conan glanced from Harpagus to the tent and back. He urgently wished for an explanation of the scene he had witnessed. Was the woman drugged, or was she under a spell? Were the Zamorians carrying her off? If so, whither? From the few words she had spoken, Conan thought the woman must be a high-born Turanian, for her Hyrkanian speech was accent-free.

Conan was, however, sufficiently seasoned in plots and intrigues not to utter his suspicions. First, his assumptions might be wrong; the woman's presence might be perfectly legitimate. Secondly, even if a plot were afoot, Harpagus would concoct a dozen plausible lies to explain his actions. Thirdly, while Conan had no fear of the small Zamorians, he did have scruples against picking a quarrel with men with whom he had just eaten and whose hospitality he had enjoyed.

Conan decided to wait until the others had bedded down for the night and then have a look in the tent. Although the Zamorians had been friendly, his barbarian instincts told him that something was amiss. For one thing, there was no sign of the usual stock-in-trade that such a party of merchants would normally carry with them. Also, these people were too silent and secretive for ordinary merchants, who, in Conan's experience, would chatter about prices and boast to one another of their sharp bargainings.

Conan's years in Zamora had given him an abiding mistrust of the folk of that nation. They were an ancient, long-settled civilized folk and, from what he had seen of them, notably given to evil. The King, Mithridates VIII, was said to be a drunkard manipulated by the various priesthoods, who struggled and competed with one another for control of the king.

As the evening progressed, one Zamorian produced a stringed instrument and twanged a few cords. Three others joined him in a wailing song, while Harpagus sat in silent dignity. Then a Zamorian asked:

"Can you give us a song, stranger?"

Conan shook his head with a shamefaced grin. "I am no musician. I can shoe a horse, scale a cliff, or split a skull; but I've no skill at singing."

The others persisted in urging him until at last Conan took the instrument and plucked the strings. "Forsooth," he said, "this thing is not unlike the harps of my native land." In a deep bass, he launched into a song:

> "We're born with sword and axe in hand,
> For men of the North are we. . . ."

When Conan finished, Harpagus asked: "In what language did you sing? I know it not."

"The tongue of the Æsir," said Conan.

"Who are they?"

"A nation of northern barbarians, far from here."

"Are you one of that tribe?"

"Nay, but I have dwelt amongst them." Conan handed the instrument back and yawned elaborately to cut off further questions. "It's time I were abed."

As if inspired by Conan's example, the Zamorians, yawning in their turn, composed themselves for sleep—all but the one told off for sentry duty. Conan wrapped himself in his blanket, lay down with his head pillowed on his saddle, and closed his eyes.

When the gibbous moon had risen well above the eastern horizon and the four Zamorians were snoring lustily, Conan cautiously raised his head. The sentry paced slowly around the encampment with spear on shoulder. Conan noted that, on the northern side of the rise, for a considerable time during every round of the camp, the sentry passed out of sight.

The next time the sentry disappeared, Conan slid to his feet and, stalking in a crouch, approached the tent, moving as silently as a shadow. The fire had burned down to a bed of coals.

"You find it difficult to sleep?" purred a Zamorian voice behind him. Conan whirled, to find Harpagus standing in the light of the rising moon. Even Conan's keen barbarian senses had not heard the man's approach.

"Yes—I—it is a mere call of nature," growled Conan.

Harpagus clucked sympathetically. "Sleeplessness can be a grave affliction. I will see to it that you sleep soundly the rest of the night."

"No potions!" exclaimed Conan sharply. He had a vision of being drugged or poisoned.

"Fear not, good sir; I had no such thing in mind," said

Harpagus gently. "Do but look closely at me."

Conan's eyes met those of the Zamorian. Something in the man's gaze riveted the Cimmerian's attention and held it captive. Harpagus' eyes seemed to grow strangely large and luminous. Conan felt as if he were suspended in a black, starless space, with nothing visible saved those huge, glowing eyes.

Harpagus slowly passed the prismatic gem in his ring back and forth in front of Conan's face. In a hypnotic monotone the Zamorian murmured: "You shall go back to sleep. You shall sleep soundly for many hours. When you awaken, you shall have forgotten all about the Zamorian merchants you encamped with. You shall go back to sleep. . . ."

Conan awoke with a start to find the sun high in the heavens. He rolled to his feet, glaring wildly, and shook the air with his curses. Not only were the Zamorians and their animals gone, but his horse had vanished also. His saddle and saddle bags still lay on the ground where he had made his rude bed, but the little leather bag of gold pieces was missing from his wallet.

The worst of it was that he could not remember whom he had companied with the previous night. He recalled the journey from Aghrapur and the fight with the swamp cat. The remains of the campfire and the traces of riding animals proved that he had shared the high ground with several other persons, but he had no memory of who they were or what they had looked like. He had a fleeting recollection of singing a song, accompanied by a borrowed stringed instrument; but the people whom he had serenaded were less than insubstantial shadows in his memory. There had been such folk, of that he was certain; but he recalled no detail of their clothing or countenances.

He remembered that he was on his way to Sultanapur. So, after venting his rage on the indifferent wilderness, he shouldered his burdens and grimly set out northward, tramping through the crowding reeds with saddle bags slung over one massive shoulder and his saddle balanced on the other. If he could no longer navigate by sun and stars, being afoot, he could at least follow the trail of his erstwhile companions by the track they had left through the trampled reeds.

III. The Blind Seer

Four days after Conan's encounter with the Zamorians, a heavy knock sounded on the door of the house of Kushad the Seer, in the port city of Sultanapur. When Kushad's daughter swung open the portal, she started back in alarm.

Before the door stood a haggard giant of a man, unshaven and mud-caked, carrying a saddle, a pair of saddle bags, a bow in its case, and a blanket roll. Although he presented a horrific aspect, the man grinned broadly through sweat and dirt.

"Hail, Tahmina!" he croaked. "You've grown since I saw you last; in a few years you'll be a woman, ripe for the plucking. Don't you know me?"

"Can it be—you must be Captain Conan, the Cimmerian!" she stammered. "Come in! My father will rejoice to see you."

"He may be less joyful when he hears my story," grunted Conan, setting down his burdens. "How fares the old fellow?"

"He is well, though his sight is nearly gone. He has no client at the moment, so come with me."

Conan followed the girl back to a chamber in which a small, white-bearded man sat cross-legged on a cushion. As Conan entered, the man stared from eyes clouded by cataract.

"Are you not Conan?" said the old man. "I discern your form but not your features. No other man has so shaken my house with the weight of his tread."

"I am indeed Conan, friend Kushad," said the Cimmerian. "You told me once that if I were ever on the dodge, I could seek asylum here."

Kushad chuckled. "So I did; so I did. But it was only a fair return for saving me from that gang of young ruffians. I recall how you scoffed at the notion that you, now a full captain in His Majesty's forces and a pillar of the kingdom, should ever again be forced to flee and hide. But you seem to draw trouble as offal attracts flies. Sit down and tell me what mischief you have been up to now. You do not require me to employ my astral vision for the finding of a lost coin, I trust?"

"Nay; but to find a whole sackful of them and a fine horse as well," growled Conan. While Tahmina went to fetch a jug of wine, Conan related his misadventure with Narkia, his flight from Aghrapur, and his encounter with the Zamorians.

"The strange thing was," he continued, "that for two whole days I could not remember with whom I had spent the night on that knoll. The memory was wiped clean from my mind, as by some devilish enchantment. Then yesterday, the scenes began to return, a little at a time, until I could picture the whole encounter. What, think you, befell me?"

"Hypnotism," said Kushad. "Your Zamorian must be skilled in the art—a priest or sorcerer, mayhap. Zamora crawls with them as does an inn with bedbugs."

"I know," grunted Conan.

"You displayed great resistance to the sorcerer's wiles, or you would not remember the Zamorians even now. You Westerners lack the fatalism that ofttimes palsies the will of us of the East. Yet I can teach you to guard yourself against such manipulation. Tell me more of these so-called Zamorian merchants."

Conan described the group, adding: "Besides, there was a woman in the tent, who came forth to warm her hands at the fire but was ordered back by the leader, Harpagus. She acted like one demented or under an enchantment."

Kushad's eyebrows arched. "A woman! What manner of female was she?"

"The light was poor; but I could see that she was tall and dark. Somewhat above thirty years of age and well-favored; wearing fluffy silken things, unsuited to—"

"By Erlik!" cried Kushad. "Know you not who the lady was?"

"Nay; who?"

"I do forget! You have been out of touch with mankind for a fortnight. Had you not heard that Jamilah, the favorite wife of King Yildiz, has been abducted?"

"No, by Crom, I hadn't! Now that I think on it, the night I fled, a company of Yildiz's horsemen galloped past without pausing to question me. I thought at first that such gentry would be searching for me on account of Orkhan's death; then I idly wondered if they were not on the trail of bigger game."

"It is your misfortune that you knew not of this kidnapping. Had you rescued the lady, your recent indiscretion would have been forgiven. His Majesty's men have turned the kingdom upside down in search of her."

"When I served at the palace," mused Conan, "I heard rumors of this favorite, but I never clapped eyes upon her. It was said that Yildiz was a simple, easy-going fellow who relied on this particular wife to make all his hard decisions. She was more king than he. I daresay the camel was her mount. But even had I rescued the lady from the Zamorians, I have no wish to continue in Yildiz's service."

"Why so?"

Conan grinned. "When I was galloping about the Hyrkanian steppe, being roasted and frozen and chased by wolves and dodging the arrows of nomads, my heart's desire was duty with the palace guard. I thought I should have naught to do but swagger about in well-polished armor and ogle the ladies."

"But when I became Captain of the Guard, I found it a terrible bore. Save for a little drill each morning, there was naught to do but stand like a statue, saluting the King and his officials, and looking for spots on the uniforms of my men. As much as anything, 'twas to escape the tedium of my post that I commenced my intrigue with that bitch Narkia.

"Besides, the unfortunate Orkhan, it appears, was a son of Tughril, High Priest of Erlik. If I know priests, he'd sooner or later find means of revenge, with or without the King's approval—poisoned needles in my bedding, or a dagger between the shoulder blades some moonless night. Anyway, two years with one master is long enough for me; especially since, as a foreigner, I could never rise to general in Turan."

"The rosiest apple oft harbors the biggest worm," said Kushad. "What would you now?"

Conan shrugged and took a gulp of Kushad's wine. "I had meant to flee to Zamora, where I know people from my old days as a thief. But the cursed Zamorians stole my horse—"

"You mean King Yildiz's horse, do you not?"

Conan shrugged. "Oh, he had horses to spare. The thieving devils got not only the beast but also the little gold I had hoarded. You it was who persuaded me to save a part of each month's pay; but see what good that's done me! I might as well have spent it on women and wine; I should then at least have pleasant memories."

"Count yourself lucky they did not cut your throat whilst you slept." Turning, Kushad called: "Tahmina!" When the girl appeared, he said: "Pull up the board and give me what lies beneath it."

Tahmina thrust a finger into a knothole in one of the floor boards and raised it. Crouching, she put an arm into the orifice and brought out a small but heavy sack. This she gave to Kushad, who handed it to Conan.

"Take what you think you'll need for a new horse, with enough besides to get you to Zamora," said the seer.

Conan untied the sack, inserted a hand, and brought out a fistful of coins. "Why do you this for me?" he asked gruffly.

"Because you were a friend when I needed a friend; and I, too, have my code of honor. Go on, take what you need instead of gaping at me like a stranded fish."

"How knew you I was gaping?"

"I see with the eyes of the mind, now that those of the body have failed me."

"I have met cursed few men in my wanderings who would do such a thing, or whom I could truly call 'friend,'" said Conan. "All the rest seize whatever they have power to take and keep whatever they can. I will pay you back when I am able."

"If you can repay me, good; if not, do not fret. I have enough to see me through this life. Daughter, draw the curtains and fetch my tripod. I must try to perceive with the eye of the spirit whither these Zamorians have gone. Conan, my preparations will take some time. You must be hungry."

"Hungry!" roared Conan. "I could eat a horse, hair, hide, bones, and all. I haven't eaten for two days, because the loss of my beast so delayed me that I ran out of provender."

"Tahmina shall prepare you a meal, and then you may wish to patronize the bathhouse down the street. Take my old cloak and keep your face within the hood. The King's agents may be on the watch for you."

An hour and a half later, Conan returned to Kushad's house. Tahmina whispered: "Hush, Captain Conan; my father is in his trance. He said you may join him if you will do so quietly."

"Then give these boots a pull, like a good girl, will you?" said Conan, thrusting out a leg.

Carrying his boots, Conan stole into the sanctum. Kushad sat cross-legged as before, but now in front of him stood a small brass tripod supporting a tiny bowl, in which some nameless substance smoldered. A thin plume of greenish smoke spiraled up from the vessel, wavering and swaying like a ghostly serpent seeking an exit from the darkened chamber.

Conan seated himself on the floor to watch. Kushad stared blankly before him. At length the seer murmured:

"Conan, you are near. Answer not; I feel your presence. I see a small caravan crossing a sandy steppe. There are—I must position myself closer—there are four asses, three horses, and a camel. One horse, a big black stallion, serves as a pack animal. That must be your mount. The camel has a tented saddle, so I cannot see who rides within; but I suspect that it be the lady Jamilah."

"Where are they?" whispered Conan.

"On a flat, boundless plain, stretching to the horizon."

"The vegetation?"

"It is all short grass, with a few thorny shrubs. They move toward the setting sun. That is all I can tell you." Slowly the aged seer shook off his trance.

Conan mused: "They must be crossing the steppe country

between the western bourn of Turan and the Kezankian Mountains, which border Zamora. The kings of Turan talk much of extending their sway over this masterless land, to crush the nomads and outlaws who dwell there. But they have done naught. The kidnappers have moved fast; they're more than halfway to Zamora. I doubt I could catch them with the fleetest horse ere they were well within that realm. But catch them I will, to get my horse and money back—or, failing that, to wreak revenge."

"If chance enable you to rescue the lady Jamilah, by all means do so. The kingdom has need of her."

"If I can return her without losing my head in the process. But why should Zamorians abduct one of Yildiz's women? For ransom? For royal spite? If aught would stir this do-nothing king to action, that's it. And Turan's might is far greater than Zamora's."

Kushad shook his turbaned head. "I am sure the King of Zamora is not behind this. Mithridates knows the strength of his kingdom as well as we, and in any event he is but a tool of the priesthoods. The deep sleep that Harpagus cast upon you suggests the involvement of priests. Are you resolved upon going to Zamora?"

"Aye, that I am."

"Then stay hidden in my house, whilst I teach you some of the tricks of my trade."

Conan scowled. "I've always found a stout, sharp blade a better defense than magical mummeries."

"Your strong right arm failed you in the Marshes of Mehar, did it not? Now use your wits, young man! When you were stationed at Sultanapur, you told me how you had scorned the bow as an unmanly weapon until you learned its value in Turan. You will make the same discovery with the mental training that I intend to give you."

"I'll steer clear of priests and wizards," growled Conan.

"Ah, but will they steer clear of you? How can you avoid them if you do pursue them to recover your property?"

Conan grunted. "I understand your meaning."

"Where you are going, you will need every shaft your quiver can hold. You may wonder how Harpagus and his confederates could so easily escape from Turan. Had a squad of the King's men caught up with them, Harpagus and his ilk could readily have cast an illusion to send their pursuers haring off in the opposite direction. And they could do the same to you."

"Uh," said Conan suspiciously. "What is it that you propose to teach me?"

Kushad smiled. "Merely to defend yourself against the occult wiles of others. I cannot cast an illusion quite so well as when I had the full sight of my orbs, yet I lack not all resource. Let us step out into the garden for a moment." When Conan had followed the seer out into the flower and vegetable garden in back of the house, Kushad turned and said: "Look at me!"

Conan stared and found that Kushad's nearly blind eyes caught and held his vision as firmly as had the sharp eyes of Harpagus. Kushad waved a hand to and fro, muttering softly.

Of a sudden, Conan found himself standing in a dense jungle, among the massive boles of orchid-hung trees, whose buttressed roots spread writhing across the jungle floor. A sound as of sawing wood caused him to whirl, hand on his sword hilt. Ten paces off, the head of a huge tiger protruded from a patch of long grass. With a low rumble, the tiger drew back its lips in a snarl, showing fangs like curved Zuagir daggers. Then it charged.

Conan whipped out his scimitar. To his horror, he felt sentient life within his grasp. Staring, he saw that he held, not a curved Turanian saber, but the neck of a writhing serpent. The snake's head strained this way and that as it sought to flesh its needle-like fangs in Conan's hand and wrist.

With a yell of revulsion, Conan hurled the serpent from him and threw himself sideways, out of the path of the tiger's hurtling body. His hand sought his dagger. Knowing how puny was the strength of even the strongest man compared to that of a giant cat, he was sure that death, which he had narrowly foiled so often, had at last caught up with him. . . .

He found himself lying among the shrubs of Kushad's garden. Grumbling, he staggered to his feet.

"See you what I mean?" said the blind seer, smiling thinly. "I must be more circumspect with my illusions; you nearly took my head off when you threw your sword. Happen I had you at a disadvantage, for you are fatigued from your recent journey. Go; you will find a bed prepared.

Tomorrow we shall begin our lessons."

"Are you ready?" said Kushad, as sunbeams played among the trellises of the garden. "Remember your numbers, and clutch the mental picture of this courtyard firmly in your mind. Now look!"

Kushad waved a hand and muttered. The small court faded away. Conan stood on the edge of a boundless swamp, lit by the eery crimson light of a setting sun. Yellowed patches of swamp grass and dried reeds alternated with pools and meres of still waters, lying jet-black beneath the bloody reflection of the scarlet eye of heaven. Strange flying creatures, like gigantic bats with lizard heads, soared overhead.

Directly in front of Conan, a huge reptilian head, as large as that of the bull aurochs whose neck Conan had broken as a stripling in Cimmeria, parted the surface of the slimy, stagnant water. As the gigantic head reared up against the red disk of the sun, there seemed to be no end of the serpentine neck supporting it. Up—up—up it went. . . .

At first sight of the creature, Conan's hand instinctively flew to his sword. But then he recalled that his weapon was within the house; Kushad had insisted that he face his trial unarmed.

Still the head rose on its colossal neck, until it towered upward thrice the height of a man. Frantically searching the shards of his memory to piece together the seer's teachings, Conan concentrated on the picture of Kushad's garden, with the small, white-bearded seer sitting placidly on a cushion laid beside the path. Little by little, the image solidified and merged with that of the actual courtyard. Conan muttered to himself, "Four threes are twelve; four fours are sixteen; four fives. . . ."

Slowly the swamp and its reptilian denizens faded from view, and Conan found himself back in Kushad's garden. He drew his sleeve across his sweat-beaded forehead, saying: "I feel as if I had been fighting a battle for an hour."

"Labor of the mind can be as strenuous as that of the body," said Kushad gently. "You are learning, my son, but you were slow to bring your mental forces to bear. We must try again."

"Not just yet, pray," said Conan. "I am fordone, as if I had run ten leagues."

"You may rest for the nonce. What will you call yourself henceforth?"

"Call myself?" snorted Conan. "What's the matter with Conan of Cimmeria?"

"Be not wroth. If there be not a price on your head now, there soon will be. A client full of bazaar gossip reports that you are accounted Jamilah's abductor, since you and she both vanished on the self-same night."

"Going under a false name is cowardly; and besides, I'm sure to forget to answer to it."

"One gets used to an assumed name sooner than one thinks. Anyway, you needs must take another identity, at least until you reach a land where your repute has not preceded you. What name would you choose—something not incongruous with your aspect?"

Conan, scowling, pondered. At last he said: "My father was Nial the smith. He was a good man."

"Excellent! You shall be Nial, at least for the nonce. Tahmina! I sense that our guest hungers again. Fetch him wherewith to stay his pangs."

"You must think I eat enough for three," said Conan, sinking large white teeth into the loaf the girl proffered. "I am still making up for my dinnerless detour through the Marshes of Mehar. Thank you, Tahmina." He took a gulp of ale.

"Captain Conan," said the girl, "I—I had a dream last night, which perchance concerns you."

"What's this, my young seeress?" asked Kushad. "Why did you not inform us sooner?"

"'Tis the first chance I have had, with you two locked in talk and saying you would fain not be disturbed."

"What of your dream, girl?" said Conan. "I scoff not at such portents; too many prophetic dreams have visited my kin."

"I dreamt I saw you running down a tunnel, deep inside the earth. Some creature did pursue you. It was too dark to see aright, but the thing was big—as large as an ox. As you ran, it gained upon you."

"Tell me more, my little one," persisted Conan. "Describe it in detail."

"I—I cannot, save that it had glowing eyes. There were eight such eyes, gleaming like great fiery jewels."

"Perhaps a pack of famished wolves?" suggested Conan.

"Nay, it was a single creature. But it did not move the way a large animal normally moves. It—I know not how to say it—it seemed to scurry along like a walking nightmare. And it came closer and closer, and I knew that in an instant it would catch you. . . ."

"Well?" barked Conan. "What then?"

"Then I awoke. That is all."

Kushad questioned his daughter, but elicited no further information. He said: "So, young Nial, meseems the dream is a symbol of something; but of what? Dreams can be interpreted in many ways, and any way may be right. Mayhap you had better avoid subterranean tunnels, in case this were a premonition of some real, material menace. Now, if you have eaten, we shall begin another trial of your powers of psychical resistance."

Several days later, Conan, wearing Kushad's hooded cloak, led his new horse to the seer's portal. The beast was a shaggy, stocky, Hyrkanian pony, shorter in the leg than the stolen Egil. Conan knew that, while the animal could easily be outdistanced by the slender-legged western breeds, it offset this shortcoming by endurance and an ability to thrive on coarse and scanty fare.

He bade Kushad and his daughter a brisk but affectionate farewell. Tahmina smiled bravely and wiped away a trembling tear. In a way, Conan was glad to leave. The young girl, whose form had just begun to fill out, had been casting sheep's eyes at him; and from a remark by Kushad, the Cimmerian gathered that the old man would welcome him as a son-in-law, if Conan ever gave up his wild, headstrong ways, got on the right side of the law, and settled down in Sultanapur to wait for the child to reach a marriageable age.

But Conan had no intention of settling down, or of tying himself to any woman. Neither did his sense of honor permit him to take advantage of Tahmina's girlish infatuation. So it was with a small sigh of relief that he strapped his gear to Ymir, his new horse, embraced his mentor and his youthful hostess, tightened the girth, and trotted smartly off.

IV. The Golden Dragon

Westward Conan wended his way at the steady pace of the seasoned rider: walk, trot, canter, trot, walk, over and over. Every third day he paused long enough to give his steed several solid hours of grazing. Failure to do this, he knew, would wear the animal out and perhaps even kill it before he arrived at his destination.

He had reached the short-grass country of western Turan, where the plain glowed with clumps of wildflowers of scarlet and gold and blue, while the air above the greensward quivered with the flutter of countless iridescent butterflies. Here the land stretched for leagues with only slight rolls and undulations. The traveler in these parts came upon few signs of human life, save an occasional neatherd with his cattle or a shepherd with his flock. Once or twice a day, Conan encountered a caravan of camels sounding the silvery tinkle of bells, and the creaking leather and jingling mail of hired horse guards. More rarely, a lone trader jogged along on his ass, leading another piled with his gear and stock of goods.

Soon, Conan knew, he would reach the border. There King Yildiz's blockhouses and patrols warded the kingdom against the nomads and outlaws who roamed the unclaimed prairie to the west. The protection they afforded the kingdom was far from perfect. One of Conan's first assignments after promotion to a regular army unit had been to chase marauders back into this sparsely-settled west country. Sometimes the troop caught the raiders and rode proudly back to their fort with severed heads on their lances. More often the pillagers gave them the slip; and they returned on lathered steeds, with glum looks on their faces and grim jokes on their lips.

The border guards, Conan was well aware, had other duties, too. They questioned all travelers who sought to enter or leave the kingdom and apprehended felons and persons wanted by the authorities. The road that Conan followed had dwindled to a sandy track; and for a mounted man there was scant choice between this track and the boundless virgin prairie. After some deliberation Conan decided not to try to bluff his way past the border guard, but to detour around the blockhouse. So he angled northwest and soon lost sight of the beaten way.

The following afternoon, a black speck atop a nearby rise attracted his attention. Approaching, he discovered a pile of rocks, which betimes the kings of Turan ordered erected to define the bounds of the kingdom. But so vague was the site of the border that the cairn might be a dozen leagues beyond, or half a dozen short, of the line that appeared on the maps in Aghrapur.

Conan continued westward, and that evening staked out his horse to graze and stretched himself upon his blanket, assured that he was now beyond the bourn of Turan.

A stealthy footstep awakened him; but, before he could spring to his feet, something clinging fell upon him. When he struggled up, it tripped and hampered him. It was a game net, such as the Hyrkanians used in their periodic mass hunts. Before he could fight his way out of the entanglement, a club smashed down upon his head, bringing a shower of shooting stars followed by blackness.

When Conan regained consciousness, he found that his wrists were firmly lashed behind him. Looking up, he saw a circle of men in the King's uniforms, some mounted and some afoot, surrounding him in the starlight. One, bearing the insignia of a Turanian officer, commanded, "On your feet, vagabond!"

Grunting, Conan rolled over and tried to rise. He discovered that, when a man is lying down with his hands tied behind him, it is difficult or even impossible for him to arise without assistance. After several tries, he sank back on the grass.

"Someone will have to boost me up," he growled.

"Help him, Arslan," said the officer. "Aidin, stand ready with your club in case he tries to bite or run."

On his feet at last, Conan roared: "What is the meaning of this? It's an outrage on a harmless traveler!"

"We shall see about that," said the officer. "Honest travelers stop for questioning at the border post, which you obviously avoided. Luckily, we had word from a shepherd who saw you straying from the road, and the night was clear enough to track you down. Now come along, and we shall learn just how harmless you are."

A trooper slipped a Hyrkanian lasso—a pole with a running noose on the end—over Conan's head and tightened it around the Cimmerian's neck. The troopers mounted and set out across the steppe, one leading Ymir while Conan stumbled along on foot.

At the blockhouse, the soldiers pushed Conan into a small, crowded room. Six men with ready weapons watched him, while their commanding officer settled himself at a rough trestle table.

"Here's the blackguard, Captain," said the lieutenant who had brought Conan in.

"Did he put up a fight?" asked the captain.

"Nay; we caught him sleeping. But I do not think—"

"Never mind what you do or do not think," snapped the captain. "You, fellow!"

"Yes?" snarled Conan, staring at the officer through narrowed lids.

"Who are you?"

"Nial, a soldier of Turan."

"You are no Hyrkanian; that is plain from your aspect and barbarous accent. Whence came you?"

"I am a native of the Border Kingdom," said Conan, who had rehearsed his lies on the trek back to the blockhouse.

"What land is that?"

"A country far to the northwest, near Hyperborea."

"In what unit of the army do you serve?"

"Captain Shendin's cuirassiers, stationed at Khawarizm."
This was a real unit and one with which Conan was familiar.
Conan was thankful now that he had, however unwillingly,
followed Kushad's advice and left most of his handsome uniform at the seer's house in Sultanapur. Had it been packed
with the rest of his belongings and had the troopers found it,
his imposture would have been shattered in an instant.

"Why are you departing from Turan? A deserter, eh?"

"Nay, I applied for leave because I learned that my aged
mother is sick at home. I am returning thither and shall be
back at my duties within three months. Send to ask Captain
Shendin if you believe me not."

"Then why did you avoid the border post?"

"So as not to waste time answering foolish questions,"
grated Conan.

The captain reddened with quick anger. As he paused
before replying, the lieutenant spoke again: "I do not think
this man can be the renegade Conan, Captain, even though
he somewhat answers the description. First, he does not
have the King's lady with him. Second, he does not try to
flatter or conciliate us, as would a guilty fugitive. And
finally, this Conan is said to have such keen senses and
mighty strength that we could not so easily have taken him
alive."

The captain pondered for a moment, then said: "Very
well; you seem to have the right of it. But I am still minded to
have him flogged for insolence and for putting us to needless
trouble."

"Pray, sir, the men are weary. Besides, if he be truly a soldier on leave—which he may well be—such a course might
cause us trouble with the commander of his unit."

The captain sighed. "Release his bonds. Next time, Master Nial, do not try such tricks upon us, and count yourself
lucky to get off without at least a beating. You may go."

Growling a surly word of thanks, Conan recovered his
sword from the soldier who held it and started for the door.
He was crowding past the troopers when another lieutenant
appeared in the hallway before him. This man's eyes
widened.

"Why, Conan!" cried the newcomer. "What do you here? Don't you remember Khusro, your old—"

Conan reacted instantly. Lowering his head in a bull-like rush, he lunged at the lieutenant, giving him so violent a push in the chest with his open hand that the man, hurled back, crashed against the wall and fell supine. Leaping over the sprawling body, Conan dashed out into the night.

Ymir was tied to a hitching post in front of the blockhouse. Without taking time to draw sword or dagger, Conan snapped the stout leather reins with a terrific jerk, vaulted into the saddle, and savagely pounded his heels against the horse's ribs.

By the time the shouting troopers had boiled out of the blockhouse, run to the paddock, saddled their mounts, and set out in pursuit, Conan was a distant speck in the starlight. As soon as a roll in the landscape hid him from view, he galloped off at right angles to the narrow road. Before the sun had thrust its ruddy limb above the level eastern horizon, he had shaken off his pursuers.

In the Zamorian language, the word *maul* denoted the most shabby, disreputable part of a city. Each of the two principal cities of Zamora, Shadizar and Arenjun, had its maul; and even some of the smaller towns boasted such unwholesome districts. The maul was an area of bitter poverty; a slum of tumble-down old houses ripe for razing; a section of starving folk defeated by life and sinking into oblivion; a quarter for new arrivals, fresh from the village and desperately struggling for a foothold in the life of the community; a haunt of thieves and outlaws who preyed alike on the rich outside the maul and on the poor within; and the repository of ill-gotten wealth.

The stench of the winding alleys of the maul of Shadizar brought Conan vivid memories of his days as a thief in Zamora. Although he had adapted himself to a soldier's life during the past two years, the smell of the maul in his nostrils roused the lawless devil in his blood. He felt a nostalgic yearning for the days when he owed no master and yielded to no discipline, save as his vestigial conscience and barbaric sense of honor dictated. Impatient of all restraint, he had often thought, during his employment as a mercenary, that

the perfect freedom he dreamed of was worth the periods of
starvation he had suffered as a thief.

Following directions received at Eriakes's Inn, Conan
strode through the forbidding alleys, lit feebly by cressets
and lamps set into the walls at distant, irregular intervals.
His boots squidged in mud and refuse as he brushed aside
beggars and pimps. A couple of knots of bravos eyed him
with hostile or predatory stares. When he scowled at them,
they turned away; his towering size and the stout scimitar at
his side dissuaded them from their felonious intentions.

He reached a doorway over which, illumined by a pair of
smoking cressets, hung a dark board on which a yellow
dragon was crudely depicted. The sign identified the Golden
Dragon, a wineshop and alehouse. Shouldering his way in,
Conan swept the common room with his wary glance.

Suspended from the low, soot-blackened ceiling, a pair of
brass lamps, burning liquid bitumen, cast a cheerful glow.
At the tables and benches sat the usual raffish crowd: a pair
of drunken soldiers, loudly boasting of herculean feats of
venery; a trio of desert Zuagirs in kaffiyyas, who revealed
by nervous sidelong glances that they were strange to cities;
a poor mad creature talking to himself in an endless mumbling monotone; a well-dressed man who, Conan guessed,
was the head of a local syndicate of thieves; a dedicated
astrologer working celestial calculations on a sheet of
papyrus. . . .

Conan headed for the counter, behind which stood a
brawny middle-aged woman. "Is Tigranes in?" he asked.

"He just stepped out. He'll be back soon. What will you
have?"

"Wine. The ordinary."

The woman uncovered a tub, dipped up a scoop, and filled
a leathern drinking jack, which she pushed toward Conan.
The Cimmerian put down a coin, took his change, and surveyed the room. Only one seat was vacant, at a small table
for two. The other occupant was a young Zamorian, slight
and dark, who stared unseeingly over his mug of ale. Conan
walked to the table and sat down. When the young man
frowned at him, he growled: "Mind?"

The youth shook an unwilling head. "Nay; you are welcome."

Conan drank, wiped his mouth, and asked: "What's news in Shadizar these days?"

"I know not. I have just come from the North."

"Oh? Tell me, then, what news from the North?"

The young man grunted. "I was in the temple guard at Yezud, but the god-rotted priests have dismissed all the native guardsmen. They say Feridun will hire only foreigners, curse him." With a glance at Conan, the Zamorian added, "Excuse me, I see you are a foreigner. Naught personal."

"It matters not. Who is Feridun?"

"The High Priest of Zath."

Conan searched his memory. "Is not Zath the spider-god of Yezud?"

"Aye."

"But why should the priesthood prefer to be guarded by foreigners?"

The Zamorian shrugged. "They say they want men of larger stature, but I suspect some power maneuver in the ceaseless war of the priesthoods."

"So they're knifing one another in the back as usual?"

"Aye, verily! For the moment, the priests of Urud have the ear of the King, and the priests of Zath are fain to oust them and usurp their place."

"In a confrontation between the Zathites and the King," mused Conan, "perchance the Zathites think they would find foreign mercenaries more trustworthy than native Zamorians. What do you now?"

"Look for employment. I am Azanes the son of Vologas, and I have been thought a good man of my hands, even though I lack your bulk. Do you know of any openings?"

Conan shook his head. "I, too, have just arrived in Shadizar the Wicked; so I am in as fine a fix as you. They say the Turanians are recruiting mercenaries in Aghrapur—hold; there's the man I came to see."

Conan gulped his wine, rose, and returned to the counter, where a bald, potbellied fellow had taken the place of the brawny matron. Conan said: "Hail, Tigranes!"

The bald man, beaming, started to cry: "Co——" but Conan stopped him with an upraised hand. "My name is Nial," he said, "and forget it not. How do you? You still had hair on your pate when last I saw you."

"Alas, it's gone the way of all things mortal, friend. How

long have you been in Shadizar? Where dwell you? How did you find me?"

"One at a time," grinned Conan. "First, let's find a place where we can talk less publicly."

"Right you are. Atossa!" When the woman took Tigranes's place behind the counter, Tigranes grasped Conan by the elbow and steered him into a curtained cubicle behind the counter.

"This one is on the house," he said, pouring two goblets of wine. "Now tell me about yourself. What have you been doing the last few years?"

"I've been a soldier in Turan, but I had to leave in haste."

The taverner chuckled. "Same old Conan—I mean Nial. Where are you staying?"

"At Eriakes's Inn, on the edge of the maul. I asked after you, and they directed me hither."

"What are you doing now?"

"Looking for gainful employment, honest or otherwise."

"If you seek a fence to dispose of your loot, do not look at me! I gave all that up after the Chief Inquisitor had me arrested. I escaped the scaffold only by bribing him with all I'd saved, to the last farthing. Well, *almost* to the last farthing." Tigranes cast a significant glance toward the curtained doorway.

Conan shook his head. "I've had enough of that starveling life, save as a last resort. But I have soldiered all the way from Shahpur to Khitai, and that should count for something."

"Speaking of Turan," said Tigranes, "a party of Turanians was here yesterday, asking questions. They said they were looking for a man of your description, accompanied by a woman. Has that aught to do with you?"

"It might or it might not. How looked these Turanians?"

"The leader was a short, square fellow with a little gray beard, who called himself Parvez. He had several fellow countrymen in tow, and an escort of a brace of King Mithridates's guards. His snooping evidently has our King's approval."

"I know who Parvez is," said Conan. "One of Yildiz's diplomats. A gang of Zamorians abducted Yildiz's favorite wife, and the king is frantic for her return. I had naught to do with that jape, but the Turanians seem to think I did.

Methinks I had better shake the dust of Shadizar from my boots."

"That were not the only reason," said Tigranes. "The law remembers you all too well, despite the years you have been away. And your size makes you conspicuous, no matter by what name you call yourself." Tigranes's eyes narrowed speculatively, and the demon of greed peered out from his small, piglike orbs.

"I had thought of going to—" began Conan, but paused as suspicion crackled in his mind. His experience with the Zamorian underworld had taught him that the "honor amongst thieves," to which the denizens of the Maul paid lip service, was in fact as rare as fur on serpents or feathers on fish.

"No matter," he said negligently. "I'll remain in hiding here for a few days ere I decide upon my next move. I shall visit you again."

Concealing his apprehension with a rough jest, Conan left the Golden Dragon and returned to Eriakes's Inn. Instead of going to bed, he roused Eriakes, paid his scot, got his horse from the stable, and by dawn was well away on the road to Yezud.

Next morning Tigranes, who had mulled things over during the night, went to the nearest police post. He told the sergeant that the notorious Conan, wanted for sundry breaches of Zamorian law in years gone by as well as for questioning by the Turanian envoy, was to be found at Eriakes's Inn.

But when the sergeant with a squad of regulars invaded Eriakes's establishment, they found that Conan had departed hours before, leaving no word of his destination. Thus Tigranes, instead of an informer's fee, received a beating for tardiness in reporting his news. Nursing his bruises, he returned to his inn, vowing vengeance on the Cimmerian, whom he illogically blamed for his mishap.

Meanwhile, Conan sped north on Ymir as fast as he dared to push his sturdy steed.

At Zamindi, the villagers were preparing for a spectacle. All the folk, in their patched brown and gray and rusty black woollens, had turned out; some boosted their children to their shoulders, the better to view the event. The much-anticipated spectacle was the burning of Nyssa the witch.

The old woman had been tied to a dead tree a bowshot from the outskirts of the town. In a ragged shift, her white hair blowing, she watched in sullen silence as a dozen men piled sticks and faggots around her. The ropes bound her tightly, but they did not sink into her flesh only because her withered form retained no fat beneath her mottled skin.

So intent upon the sight were the villagers that none remarked the clop of hooves along the path that led from the road to Shadizar. As the headman thrust his torch into the pile of firewood, the horse, a stocky Hyrkanian sorrel, nosed his way among the rearmost members of the crowd.

The smaller sticks caught fire and blazed up with a cheerful crackle. Nyssa looked down silently, her rheumy old eyes glazed with resignation.

Feeling a nudge and hearing a snuffling sound, one villager, munching an apple, turned and recoiled. The nudge was from the velvety nose of Ymir, who was begging for a bite of the apple. The man's startled gaze traveled along the horse's back to encompass a giant figure astride the beast. Conan rasped:

"What goes on here?"

"We burn a witch," replied the man shortly, with a scowl of suspicion.

"What has she done?"

"Put a curse upon us, that's what, so three children and a cow died, all in the same night. Who are you, stranger, to question me?"

"Had there been a feud between you?"

"Nay, if it be any of your affair," replied the man testily. "She used to be our healer; but some devil possessed her and caused these deaths."

The larger faggots were now catching fire, and the rising smoke made Nyssa cough.

"Men and beasts die all the time," ruminated Conan. "What makes you think these deaths unnatural?"

The man turned to confront Conan. "Look you, stranger, you mind your business whilst we mind ours. Now get along, if you would not be hurt!"

Conan had no love of witches. Neither had he any idea of

civilized laws and rules of evidence. But still it seemed to him that the villagers were venting their grief on the aged crone more because she was old, ugly, and helpless than because they had reason to think her guilty. The Cimmerian seldom interfered in others' affairs where neither honor drove nor profit beckoned. If the villager had spoken him fair, he might have shrugged and gone his way.

But Conan was impulsive and easily roused to anger. And the protection of women, regardless of age, form, or station, was one of the few imperatives of his barbarian code. The villager's threat tipped the balance in the old woman's favor.

Conan backed his horse a few steps, wheeled the animal, and rode away from the crowd. Then he swung Ymir around, swept out his scimitar, and heeled the horse. As Ymir broke into a canter, headed straight for the tree to which the witch was tied, Conan uttered a fearful scream—the ancient Cimmerian war cry.

Startled faces turned; the villagers scrambled out of the way. Several were knocked down by the plunging beast.

Reaching the fire-ringed victim, the frightened animal rolled its eyes and reared. Conan soothed Ymir as he leaned into the smoke to smite the bindings that encircled the tree. The strands parted easily, for the villagers had thriftily chosen old and rotten rope for the burning.

As a collective growl arose from the thwarted peasants, Conan extended his free arm, roaring: "Catch hold, grandmother!"

Nyssa seized the brawny forearm and clung to it as, with a mighty heave, Conan swung her up on the horse's withers, before the saddle.

"Hold on!" shouted Conan, pressing the oldster against his chest and urging Ymir into a run again.

Once more the crowd, which had started to converge and advance, parted and scattered. Even as Conan plowed through them, he saw some of the more active men run to their crofts. As Ymir carried his double burden away from the village, Conan glanced back. Raging, the men were reëmerging with scythes, pitchforks, and a couple of spears.

"Where do you want to go?" Conan asked the witch.

"I have no home to call my own," she replied in a quavery voice. "They have already burned my hut."

"Then whither?"

"Pray, whither you go, sir."

"I'm bound for Yezud; but I cannot take you with me all the way."

"If you will return to the main road and turn left, you will soon come upon another track, which leads uphill to my hiding place. Though I know not if your horse can bear the both of us up so steep a slope."

"Can he walk if I lead him?"

"Aye, sir; of that I am sure. But hurry! I do hear the dogs barking behind us."

A distant baying wafted to Conan's ears. Keen though his senses were, those of the old woman had earlier identified the sound.

"Your hearing is good for one of your years," he remarked.

"I have ways of reinforcing my mortal senses."

"If they have set dogs after us, what's to stop them from following us to your hideaway?"

"Let me but once reach the place, and I have means to lead them astray."

As they came out upon the main road, the sounds of pursuit grew louder, for Ymir was slowed by the weight of his double burden. Another quarter-hour, and Nyssa indicated the track to her refuge.

For a while, Ymir trotted up the steep path, which rose and dipped and wound through broken country. The baying increased apace, and Conan more and more disliked the situation. On the flat, with room to maneuver, he did not fear a villageful of yokels armed with improvised weapons. But on this uncertain footing, if the pursuers were brave enough to close in even after he had slain the foremost, they could swarm around him, hamstring his mount, and cut him to pieces.

"Those fellows must have horses," he muttered between clenched teeth.

"Aye, sir; the village breeds them and has a score of the beasts. And the lads are spry afoot; they beat the other villages in foot races at every fair. I used to be proud of my village."

Conan knew that, if he abandoned Nyssa, he could escape his pursuers even if they tried to run him to earth after they had recaptured the aged witch. But having committed himself to the crone's rescue, he gave no thought to any other course. In such matters he could be obstinate indeed.

The track thrust upward, ever steeper and more rugged. Conan pulled up and swung off the weary horse, saying: "I'll walk; you ride. How much farther goes this path?"

"A quarter of a league. Near the end, I needs must also walk."

On they plodded, Conan leading Ymir by the reins, while behind them the baying waxed louder as men and dogs gained on their quarry. Conan expected to sight their pursuers at any time.

"Here I must dismount," quavered Nyssa. "Kindly help me down, good sir."

When the witch had regained her uncertain footing, she pointed up a trackless slope and started up it vigorously, although each breath she drew was inhaled as a painful gasp.

Glancing back across the waste of tumbled rock and scanty vegetation, Conan caught the ominous blink of sun on steel. He gritted: "We must move faster. Let me carry you, grandmother!"

When she protested, he swept her frail form into his strong arms and hurried up the slope. Sweat rolled down his face, and his own breath came harder.

"Through yonder notch," murmured the witch, pointing.

Still carrying the old woman and leading Ymir, Conan found himself in a narrow canyon or gully, the sides of which supported a few scrubby pines. The bottom of the gulch was a jumble of stream-rounded stones of all sizes, among which gurgled and murmured a shrunken creek. Conan had to leap from boulder to boulder, while Ymir staggered and stumbled along behind him.

"H-here!" whispered Nyssa.

Around a slight bend in the gorge, Conan sighted the mouth of a cave, all but hidden by shrubs and overhanging vines. As the woman sank down, gasping, Conan said:

"Cast your spell quickly, grandmother; for the villagers are close upon our heels."

"Help me to start a fire," she wheezed.

Conan gathered some dry leaves and small sticks and started a little blaze with flint and steel. Then he turned to speak to Nyssa, but she had disappeared into the cave.

Soon she tottered out to the fire again, carrying a leathern bag in one bony fist. This she opened and, from one of its many internal compartments, extracted a pinch of powder, which she sprinkled on the blaze. As the fire flared and sputtered, a curious purple smoke arose, twisting and writhing like a serpent in its death throes. In a low voice, she muttered an incantation in a dialect so archaic that Conan could catch no more than a word or two.

"Hasten, grandmother," he growled, cocking an ear toward the ever-rising tumult of the pursuit. "They'll be upon us any time, now."

"Interrupt me not, boy!" she snapped. It had been years since anyone had dared thus to address Conan, but he meekly submitted to the affront.

From where he sat on a boulder, Conan could sight the end of the gorge, where it opened out into the broader valley up which they had ascended. As his eyes caught a flash of motion, he sprang to his feet and swept out his scimitar. In so narrow a cleft, his foes could come at him only one or two at a time—provided they did not scale the cliff to attack him above, or to get behind him, and provided they had no bows and arrows. Conan was wearing no armor, and he knew that not even his pantherlike agility would enable him to dodge arrows loosed at close range.

Nyssa was still muttering over the fire, when Conan snarled: "Here they come!"

"Speak not, and put away that sword," quavered the witch. "Now look again!" she said with a note of triumph in her shrill old voice.

Conan stared. The peasants and their dogs were streaming past the mouth of the gully.

"Hold your tongue, boy, and they'll not hear us!" she hissed.

Soon the rush of dogs, men, and horses had swept past the mouth of the gorge, and the clatter of their passing died away.

"How did you do that, grandmother?" asked Conan in wonderment.

"I cast a glamour, so to those folk the mouth of this ravine appeared as solid rock. If you had shouted, or if the flash of the sun on your blade had reached them, or if one of them had thrust a tool against that seeming wall of rock, the illusion would have been destroyed like a fog beneath the morning sun." She leaned back wearily against the wall of the gorge. "Help me back into the cave, I pray. I am fordone."

Conan assisted the old woman into the cavern, in which provisions, bundles of herbs, and other possessions were piled haphazardly. As she sank down, she said: "Young man, I must ask you for one more boon. Can you cook? I am too feeble even to get your supper."

"Aye, I can cook in my own fashion," said Conan. "It will be no banquet royal, I assure you; but I've camped alone in the wilds often enough to know the rudiments." He rummaged among the witch's supplies, then built up the smoldering fire. As he worked, he asked: "Tell me, grandmother, what befell between you and the village?"

She coughed, caught her breath, and spoke: "I am Nyssa of Komath. For many years I have earned a scanty living as the white witch of Zamindi, curing ills of man and beast, foretelling the prospects of young lovers seeking to wed, and predicting the changing seasons. But, as I have told the folk many a time and oft, naught is certain in occult matters, and the final decisions rest ever with the gods.

"Then a disease struck Zamindi. Many were sick, and one night three bairns died. I did what I could, but neither my simples nor my spells availed me. Then voices rose against me, saying that I had cast a malignant spell.

"'Twas naught but a rumor set in motion by the headman, Babur, who long had coveted the little patch of land on which my poor hut stood. I enraged him by refusing to sell it to him, even at a reasonable price; so this is his revenge." A spasm of coughing shook her. "I cast my horoscope yestereve and saw that it portended peril. This morn I was gathering my last supplies to bring to this shelter, which I had prepared for emergencies long ago. But the villeins were too quick for me; they came and dragged me to the village." She cackled. "But you and I have cheated the omens, at least for the nonce. Now what of you, young man?"

Conan told Nyssa as much of his recent history as he thought expedient, adding: "What of my future?"

Her faded old eyes took on a faraway look. "Some things about you I already sense. You are a man of blood. Strife follows you and seeks you out, even when you would fain avoid it. There is great force about you. Nor am I the last old woman whom you will come upon in dire need and rescue." After a pause, she added: "Beware to whom or what you give your heart. Many times you will believe that you have attained your heart's desire, only to have it slip through your fingers and vanish like a puff of morning mist.

"But more of that anon. My poor old heart has been sorely strained this day, and I must needs have rest. I am not one of those who have added to their mortal span by the practice of arcane arts.

"Tomorrow I shall work a powerful conjuration for you, to try to part the veil that enshrouds the future. But meanwhile I will give you a token of my gratitude."

"You need not, grandmother—" began Conan, but she silenced him with a gesture.

"None shall say that Nyssa fails to pay her debts," she said. "'Tis but a small thing I give you, yet it is all I have to give this night, what with the hazards and confusion of this turbulent day."

She fumbled among her disorderly piles of belongings and turned again to Conan, holding a small pouch, which she pressed upon him. "This," she explained, "is a spoonful of the powder of Forgetfulness. If an enemy close in upon you, thinking he has you at his mercy, throw a pinch into his face. When he breathes this dust, 'twill be as if he had never beheld you or had knowledge of you."

"What should I do with the fellow then?" asked Conan. "If he'd wronged me, my natural wont would be to slay him; but it would seem cowardly to strike him down, and him not knowing the reason for the quarrel."

"I would say to let him go and think no more about the matter. To slay him under such conditions were like killing a babe because you quarreled with his father. A heartless sort of revenge, indeed."

Conan grunted a puzzled assent, although in fact he had never before thought about the rights and wrongs of the matter. Among his fellow Cimmerians, it was customary to seek revenge upon a member of another clan by slaying the offender's kin.

Conan was tempted to refuse the proffered pouch, claiming that he had only contempt for magic and wanted nothing to do with it. But the old woman seemed so eager for him to have her gift that he accepted it with a growl of thanks rather than hurt her feelings.

When Conan awoke the next morning, he found Nyssa's body stiff and cold. She had not cheated the omens after all.

V. *The City on the Crag*

The sun had slipped behind the humped backs of the Karpash Mountains when Conan guided Ymir into the narrow
valley that led to Yezud, city of the spider-god. The deepen-
ing shadows cast a black pall over the defile. Here little vegetation clothed the rocky soil; for the central, snow-capped
ridge of the Karpashes, stretching from north to south for a
hundred leagues without a single pass, had wrung the mois-
ture from the western winds before they swept on east to
Zamora. Ymir's shod hooves rang a metallic tattoo on the
stones, save when the horse picked his way through slippery
seepages of liquid bitumen. Below the path, a shrunken
remnant of a stream gurgled as it played hide-and-seek
among the boulders.

For the most part, the ever-rising path was wide enough to
accommodate only a single horseman. Whenever it spread
itself more generously, Conan passed knots of people wait-
ing to resume their downward passage. One trader, delayed
at such a turnout, led four asses, each laden with two bulky
casks of bitumen. In the lowlands of southern Zamora, this
dark mineral oil was put to sundry uses; it served as a purga-
tive for people, a lubricant for wagon wheels, a base for
paint, a fuel for lamps, and a cure for mange.

Conan caught up with a plodding procession of cattle,
shambling upward on the path to Yezud. When the curvature

45

of the slope revealed the serpentine path ahead, Conan marveled at the size of the herd. There must, he thought, be eighty to a hundred animals, pulled or prodded along by a dozen neatherds. The sloth of the cumbersome beasts irritated the Cimmerian, since nowhere could he pass them while the narrow track continued its winding way.

Although the departure of the sun had cast black gloom within the gorge, the sky above was still a bright cerulean blue when the ravine at last opened out into a narrow plain. Here a hamlet huddled at the roadside. Beyond it, where the canyon split in twain, a walled city or acropolis perched upon the shoulder of a crag formed by the divergent gorges; and like a monarch's crown, the marble temple of Zath reared up to tower above the roseate roofs of the fortified city. This lofty citadel bore the name of Yezud, whereas the lower village or suburb was known as Khesron.

As soon as the widened path permitted, Conan cantered past the herd of cattle and trotted briskly through the huddled village, where dirty children scampered from the road and barking dogs ran out to worry Ymir's hooves. The lone public building in Khesron, rising a story above the score of other dingy structures of the community, proclaimed itself an inn by means of a branch nailed to a board above the lintel of the front door.

The Cimmerian continued onward toward the rocky shoulder on which stood the walled city of Yezud, along a steeply sloping roadway cut into the stone of the hillside. Conan perceived that the only means of entry into the citadel was this same roadway and that Yezud, if resolutely defended, would be virtually impregnable. The steep sides of the eminence, which bore the citadel aloft and which merged into Mount Ghaf behind, were so nearly vertical that only a party of Cimmerian hillmen, unencumbered by armor, could hope to scale this formidable bastion.

Ymir balked on the hillside path. Although Conan spurred him forward, the animal refused to move. At last the Cimmerian dismounted and plodded up the incline, pulling Ymir along by his bridle. All the climbing way, the horse rolled his eyes, pricked up his ears, and behaved as if he sensed some evil beyond the comprehension of his human companion.

Man and unwilling horse at last reached the small stone platform before the city portal, a dizzy height above the plain. A pair of armed men, of greater stature than most Zamorians, stood guard before the open valves of the imposing bronze-studded gates.

"Your name and business?" snapped one of the guards, eyeing Conan hardily.

"Nial, a mercenary soldier," replied Conan. "I heard that such as I are being hired."

"They *were*," replied the soldier, his lip curling slightly with the shadow of a sneer. "But no more. You have tardy come."

"You mean the places are all filled?"

"And you have had your journey all for naught." The man spoke Zamorian with an unfamiliar accent.

"Are you two amongst those lately hired, then?" asked Conan.

"Aye; we are men of Captain Catigern's Free Company."

Although nettled by the soldier's surly manner, Conan kept his outward calm. "Well then, friend, whence hail you?"

"We are Brythunians."

"Indeed? I've traveled many lands, but never yet Brythunia. I crave a word with the man who hired you, whoever he may be."

"Too late for that today. Try again in the morning."

Conan grunted. "Well, is there an inn in Yezud where I can take lodging and stable my horse?"

The soldier laughed scornfully. "Any fool knows that only the priests and those who work for them may rest their heads overnight within the walls of Yezud!"

The quick flame of Conan's anger flared up. He had been in no pleasant mood as a result of the delay occasioned by the herd of cattle and the balkiness of his mount, and now the man's insolence raised his hot temper to the boiling point. With an effort he choked off a sharp retort, but he memorized the man's face should the future provide him with a chance for retaliation. As calmly as he could, the barbarian asked:

"Where, then, do travelers lie of nights?"

"Try Bartakes's Inn in Khesron. If that be full of pilgrims, the stars must be your roof."

"They've served me thus ere now," growled Conan. He turned to find the downward path blocked by the same scrambling herd of cattle that he had passed on his upward climb to Yezud. Mooing and groaning, the animals were being prodded up the slope in single file by cursing herdsmen.

"Stand aside, lout, and let the cattle in!" barked the soldier.

Conan lips tightened and his hand itched for his sword hilt, but he remembered the flatness of his purse and held his peace. Unable to descend the path while the cattle occupied it, he waited, fuming, on the flat as the beasts were driven through the gate, one after another. Before the last animal had stumbled into the citadel and the gate slammed shut, stars had begun to twinkle in a darkling sky. Leading Ymir, Conan picked his way down the path, peering into the gloaming lest a misstep send him or his mount over the edge and down the cliffside.

Bartakes's Inn had plenty of room, because the flux of pilgrims swelled only at certain seasons of year, during the great festivals in the temple of Zath. The spring festival had come and gone, while the Festival of All Gods still lay ahead. So there were empty beds in the sleeping rooms and empty stalls in the stable.

Conan shouldered in the front door and glanced about the common room, where a few patrons sat at tables, eating, drinking, or gaming. Several were men of goodly size, with brown or tawny hair; from their garb, Conan guessed them to be members of the company of Brythunian mercenaries. Others were nondescript locals, save for one slender, swarthy fellow with a shaven head, wrapped in a monkish robe that fell below his ankles. Conan had seen such men before, in Corinthia and Nemedia, where he had been informed that they were Stygian priests, or acolytes, or simply students. This one was absorbed in his sheaf of writing material—a mixture of sheets of parchment, rolls of papyrus, and thin slabs of wood—spread out on the table before him.

Behind the counter stood a plump, wavy-haired young woman, pouring ale from a dipper into the leathern drinking jack of a patron. As Conan approached, she turned her head and called: "Father!"

A fat taverner, wiping his hands on his apron, strolled out from the kitchen. "Yes, sir?" he said invitingly.

Conan arranged for dinner and bed for himself and a bucket of grain and a stall for Ymir. He bought a stoup of ale with his meal and retired early.

The rising sun saw him again before the gates of Yezud. When the portals swung apart, Conan found himself confronting two unfamiliar guards and a man who, from his bearing and handsome equipment, appeared to be an officer. This man was massive, almost as tall as Conan, and his bristling red mustache curled upward at the ends. Seeing the Cimmerian, he said:

"Ho! You must be the fellow who came here at closing time last night, asking about a post in Yezud. There is naught here for a fighting man; my boys have taken over the protection of the citadel."

"You must be Captain Catigern," said Conan dourly.

"Aye. So?"

"Captain, I still desire to speak with the man who does the hiring. I can do a few things other than splitting skulls."

The captain studied Conan carefully, with a frown born of suspicion. "It is not likely he'll have aught for you. Are you friendly to the worship of Zath?"

"I'm friendly to all who buy my services and pay that which they promise," grunted Conan.

Lips pursed, Catigern contemplated the huge Cimmerian. Then he turned to one of the guards, saying: "Morcant! take this man to the Vicar. Let him decide whether the fellow is to be trusted within. And you, stranger, leave your sword with us until these matters are resolved."

Conan silently handed over his scimitar and followed Morcant into the city. The buildings were of severely plain design—row upon row of neat, white-washed, red-roofed shops and dwellings, hardly to be distinguished one from another. The streets were swept cleaner than any Conan had come upon in other cities; the main thoroughfare appeared impeccable despite the drove of cattle that had plodded along it but a few hours before. Conan asked Morcant:

"Yestereve I saw above eighty head of cattle entering the city. Would the folk have need of so much beef? Judging from the size of the town, it would require a month for the citizens to eat it all."

"No questions, stranger," snapped the Brythunian.

Conan darted discreet glances to right and left from beneath his heavy brows, looking for signs of a stockyard in which the cattle might be confined. But although they passed stables and workshops of all descriptions, he saw no sign of a pen or corral.

At last they reached the precinct of the temple of Zath. Conan craned his neck and stared like a yokel at the largest building he had ever beheld—an edifice even more imposing than the temples and palaces of Shadizar and Aghrapur. The structure was built of great blocks of opalescent marble, gleaming golden in the sun-washed light of morning. From the huge central nucleus projected eight wings, each bedight with mosaic-inlaid columns and pilasters. Except where broad steps led up to the main entrance, lengths of polished granite wall joined the outer end of each wing to that of its neighbors. A vast central dome towered over all, and the early morning sun reflected with blinding intensity the gold leaf that covered the dome.

Before the main portal—an enormous pair of doors embellished with bronzen reliefs—two Brythunian guards stood rigidly at attention, their crimson uniforms spotless, their mailshirts agleam, and their halberds grounded at their sides. Morcant announced:

"A man to see the Vicar."

One guard pushed open a small door let into one of the huge bronze valves of the main portal. Conan ducked under the lintel and found himself in a spacious carpeted vestibule, whence passages led off to either side. Facing the wide entranceway, another pair of giant doors, these ornamented with exquisite gilded reliefs, towered above the visitors. Before the inner doors were stationed another pair of halberd-bearing guards.

Morcant nodded to these sentinels and led Conan down one of the side passages. As they proceeded, Conan became conscious of a faint odor of carrion. This, he knew, was not uncommon in temples where animals were either sacrificed to the god or eviscerated for purposes of divination. So he paid scant attention to the disagreeable smell.

After conducting the Cimmerian through a bewildering maze of corridors, Morcant stopped at an oaken door, before which stood another Brythunian mercenary, and knocked. When a voice called: "Enter!" he opened the door and waved Conan in.

A seated figure in a white turban bent over an ornate, flat-topped desk, writing by the light of a bitumen lamp. As Conan came to attention before him, the man raised his head. "Yes, my son?"

Conan started and reached for the sword that no longer hung at his side. For the man was Harpagus, he who had cast Conan into a hypnotic sleep in the marshes of Mehar.

Harpagus gave no sign of recognition. Gathering his wits, Conan realized that, when he had encountered the Zamorians in the marshes, his face had been obscured by the turban cloth wound about his head. Even when he had shared a dinner with Harpagus and his men, he had not, because of the swarms of biting insects, removed the cloth altogether; he had merely raised the part that covered his mouth and chin and tucked it into the upper folds.

Struggling to hide the hatred that welled in his barbarian breast for the man who had tricked and robbed him, Conan forced himself to speak calmly: "I am Nial, a mercenary from the Border Kingdom. Hearing that the temple was hiring soldiers, I have come in hope of finding a post."

The turbaned man gently shook his head. "You are too late by a fortnight, my son. Captain Catigern likewise learned of the opportunity and, there being no wars at present in Brythunia, brought his Free Company hither."

"So I've been told. Nonetheless, sir, I need employment; for my money is nearly gone, and I must find more ere leaving to seek a post in other lieus."

Harpagus stroked his narrow chin. "The temple needs a clerk skilled in the casting of accounts, to keep our books. Are you a man trained to that task?"

It was Conan's turn to shake his shaggy head. "Not I! I cannot add a column of numbers twice and arrive at the same sum."

"Well, then—ah! We do have need of a blacksmith, at least for a time; since ours lies dying of a wasting distemperature. Perchance you know that skill?"

Conan's teeth flashed whitely in a sudden grin. "My father was a smith, and I was apprenticed to him for years when I was young."

"Good; excellent! You have the thews for the task, at least. You may start work today. The Brythunian will show you to your smithy, now in the care of Pariskas's bellows boy. He shall serve you in like capacity."

After settling such matters as Conan's wage, living quarters for himself, and stabling for his horse, Harpagus said: "We are then agreed, my son. But you must understand that, for those who dwell in holy Yezud, there shall be no drinking of fermented liquors, no gambling, and no fornication. And all do promise to attend the services of holy Zath at least once every ten-day." The Vicar paused, his brow furrowed. "Have I not met you on some previous occasion?"

Conan felt his nape-hairs rise, but he spoke with a negligent air. "I think not, sir—unless it were a chance encounter in Nemedia or Brythunia, where I have served as a mercenary."

Harpagus shook his head. "Nay, I have never traveled to those lands. Still, your voice reminds me of someone I knew briefly . . . No matter. Go with the guard to your new quarters. You will find enough accumulated tasks to keep you busy."

"One thing more, sir. I want my sword, now in the custody of the gate guards."

Harpagus smiled thinly. "You shall have it. Forbidding a blacksmith his weapon were like confiscating a poet's verses; he'll only make another."

As the Brythunian led Conan through the narrow streets, the Cimmerian growled: "Is the Vicar's name Harpagus?"

"Aye."

"So I thought. Did I understand him aright, that in Yezud there is no wine, nor beer, nor gambling, nor light love?"

Morcant grinned. His manner had thawed to friendliness since learning that Conan would be a fellow employee of the temple. "High Priest Feridun is a very righteous man—a dolorously righteous man, and he hopes to impose his principles on all in Zamora. We of the Free Company go down to Bartakes's Inn for our sinful amusements. Feridun would like to close down that place, too. But he does not dare, knowing that the Free Company would go on the road if such constraints were imposed upon us."

Conan gave a rumble of mirth, knowing full well that brigandage was the usual occupation of mercenary companies out of military employment; but rarely was it so plainly named.

"I see no cause for merriment," said Morcant crisply with a reproving stare.

"No offense meant," said Conan, wiping the smile from his lips. "But I've been a hired sword myself and know somewhat of the ways of mercenaries."

The smithy was a simple, one-story affair, of which the larger section, open to the street, housed a forge, while a small apartment to the left did duty as the smith's domestic quarters. As Conan entered the smithy, a Zamorian boy of perhaps twelve years, who had been perched on the anvil whittling a stick, jumped to his feet. Conan explained his presence.

"I am Lar, son of Yazdates," said the boy. "Pray, Nial sir, I hope you will teach me some smithery whilst I do work for you. The old smith would never let me handle his tools. Belike he feared I should grow up to take his post from him."

"We shall see," replied Conan. "It depends on how able a man of your hands you prove to be."

"Oh, I am very able, sir, for my age. I have practiced on the sly when old Pariskas was not looking. Sometimes he caught me at it and beat me." The boy looked apprehensively at the giant who was to be his new master.

"If I ever beat you, it won't be for trying to improve yourself," growled Conan. "Let's see to the tools."

Conan had not worked as a smith since, years before, a feud had driven him forth from his Cimmerian tribe. But, as he swung the heavy hammers and handled the stout iron tongs, he felt a thrill of familiarity. It would not be long, he felt sure, before he regained his half-remembered skill.

"Lar," he said, "I am going down to Khesron to fetch my horse and my belongings. While I'm gone, you shall start up the furnace, and we'll tackle this work today. By the way, where went all those cattle, which I saw driven into Yezud yestereve?"

"They went through a doorway on the western side of the temple," said Lar.

"A small town like this scarce needs so many beasts for food," mused Conan.

"Oh, sir, they are not meat for the townsfolk; not even the priests! They are for Zath."

"Forsooth?" said Conan. "That I can hardly believe. I have seen much of temples and more of priests. In those where the worshipers bring animals to sacrifice, the holy men slay the creatures, offer the skin and bones and offal to the god, and feast on the good flesh themselves. Why do you think your priests do not the same?"

"But, sir, everybody in Yezud knows the cattle are devoured by Zath! Have you been in the naos of the temple?"

"Not yet. What's there?"

"You will see all when you attend your first service. There stands the statue of Zath, in the likeness of a huge spider carven of black stone. Its body is enormous, and its legs—its legs . . . ." The boy broke off with a shudder.

"A statue cannot eat cattle," remarked Conan, surprised at the boy's display of fear.

"Each night the statue comes to life," the lad continued. "It descends through a trapdoor in the holy place and enters the tunnels below, where it seizes upon the animals that have been driven in to assuage its appetite. So say the priests."

Conan ruminated. "I've seen many strange things in my travels, but never a statue that came to life. Even if this tale be true, what would such a spider want with a hundred head of cattle at a time? I have never kept a spider as a pet; but I do know something of the habits of other beasts of prey. I should think one ox would suffice a creature like Zath for a fortnight at the least."

"Oh, sir, these are holy mysteries! You must not pry into that which the gods do not intend us mortals to know." As he spoke, the boy reverently bowed his head and touched his fingertips to his forehead.

Conan grunted. "That's as may be. Now start up the forge, lad, while I go to get my gear from the inn."

Some time later, leading Ymir, Conan approached the common stable where he had been allotted a stall. As Conan was instructing the stable boy in the care of Ymir, a commotion arose in one of the more distant stalls. A horse was rearing, pawing the air, and squealing frantically.

"What's that?" asked Conan.

The groom looked around. "It's that accursed black stallion the Vicar bought in Turan," he said. "We have not been able to exercise him properly, because no man durst try to ride him."

"Hm," said Conan. "I'll take a look." He strolled down to the stall of the fractious stallion and recognized Egil. The horse whinnied with delight and nuzzled him.

Not daring to address the horse directly, Conan turned to the groom. "He seems to like me, the gods know why."

The groom leaned on his shovel while his sluggish thoughts took form. At last he mumbled: "Perhaps, sir, you could ride him. Are you fain to undertake his exercising? If the priests agreed, that is."

It was on the tip of Conan's tongue to say yes; but then it struck him that, if word got back to Harpagus, the Vicar might suspect that his new blacksmith and the former owner of Egil were one and the same. Instead he replied:

"We shall see. Just now I can barely spare time to keep my own nag in condition."

VI. The Temple of the Spider

Since Yezud was provided with no inn or eating-house and
Conan did not wish to plod down to Khesron for each repast,
he made arrangements for Lar's mother to cook his meals.
At sundown, Conan washed the soot from his face and arms
and followed Lar to the small house where the boy and his
widowed mother dwelt. The house, freshly whitewashed,
was neat within and furnished in the rear with a small, well-
tended vegetable garden.

Amytis, a middle-aged woman with a weary face and
graying hair, cooked an adequate meal, albeit Conan grumbled at the lack of ale with which to wash it down. He listened in dour silence as Amytis prattled on about her
ancestry, her kin, and her well-remembered husband.

"'Twas bitter hard after he died, poor man," she sighed.
"But with the money you pay my Lar, and the stipend my
daughter earns at the temple, and the coppers I make by taking in washing, we manage."

"You have a daughter?" asked Conan, eyeing the woman
with the first faint stir of interest.

"Aye, Rudabeh is chief of the temple's dancing girls and
has other responsibilities besides. A very capable maid; the
man will be lucky who gets her to wife."

"The dancers are allowed to wed?"

"After their discharge, aye. In fact the priests approve of it; they give each girl a dowry when her service ends—if she has behaved herself, that is."

"How do they choose temple dancers?" Conan inquired idly, spooning out a portion of pudding.

"The priests hold a contest every year," explained Amytis, "to pick the two likeliest dancers. Families come from as far away as Shadizar, bringing their prettiest maidens, for the competition; but most come from the towns nearby. It is accounted an honor to have a daughter in the service of Zath."

"How long is their term of service?"

"The winners serve the temple for five years."

Conan glanced at young Lar. "Why didn't you tell me that you had a sister?"

The boy grimaced. "I did not think a great man like you would be interested in a *girl*."

Conan turned back to Amytis to hide his grin from his youthful hero-worshiper and asked: "Does your daughter ever visit you?"

"Oh, aye; four times in a month she is granted leave and comes here to sup. She spent an evening with us but three nights agone."

With an ostentatious show of unconcern, Conan yawned, stretched, and rose. "Lar," he said carelessly, "You must take me to the temple one day and explain the rituals. The Vicar commanded me to attend not less than thrice a month, and I must needs obey him."

Excusing himself, Conan returned to his smithy. He thought briefly of repairing to Bartakes's Inn to enliven the evening, but an afternoon of wielding the heavy tools of his new trade had left him more than willing to retire early.

The next day was spent at forge and anvil. While Lar manned the bellows, Conan shod several horses, welded a broken scythe blade, hammered a dent out of a helmet belonging to one of the Brythunians, and in odd moments made several score of nails. He was pleased to find the skills he had learned in boyhood so readily returning to him.

The following morning, Conan accompanied Lar to the temple of Zath, into which many dwellers of the citadel were streaming. Now the huge inner doors, as well as the outer portals, stood open to the worshipers. The halberd-bearing guards stood stiffly at attention, but their lusty glances followed many a well-favored woman who tempered her piety with smiles.

Towering above the crowd, Conan entered the naos. The odor of carrion was stronger here; one less hardened to the smell of death than the Cimmerian might have found it nauseating. The circular chamber of the naos, in the hub of the huge temple complex, was capable of accommodating thousands of the faithful. But, since this was not a time of festival, only a few hundred had foregathered in the capacious rotunda.

Conan observed that the entire floor was inlaid with delicate mosaics, skillfully patterned into the form of a series of connecting spiderwebs. Each web occupied a space scarcely larger than the width of a man's shoulders; and at the center of one web Lar took his stand, gesturing to Conan to do likewise.

Conan's appraising eye sought out the gilded piers that rose at intervals to support the lofty domed ceiling. Everywhere the spiderweb pattern was repeated. It festooned the plastered walls, wreathed around the pillars, and on a larger scale spread out across the inner surface of the gilded dome. Here the design was realized in black on white; there in white on black; elsewhere in red on blue, or gold on green, or purple on silver, or some other chromatic combination.

The glitter of gold leaf, reflecting the light of a hundred gilded lamps suspended on bronzen chains from the shadowy recesses of the ceiling, and the endless repetition of the spoked cobweb pattern induced hypnotic immobility. Conan closed his eyes to shut out the reeling lights and painted swirls and forced himself to concentrate upon the peaceful garden of the seer Kushad.

When Conan trusted himself to reopen his eyes, his gaze became fixed upon the scene before him. Partly recessed into the wall surrounding the rotunda and partly projecting into the circle of the naos stood a sacred enclosure, square in plan. This holy place, raised above the level of the floor of the naos for better viewing by the congregated faithful, was fronted by three broad marble steps, which stretched across the full width of the sacred area. A pierced railing of polished brass, the height of a woman's waist, curved forward from the bottom step to separate the sacred precinct from the section allotted the worshipers.

Above the steps and on the right side of the stage stood a massive, time-worn ebon chest fitted with bronzen clasps, green with age. This ancient container was decorated with the ubiquitous spiderwebs, formed by slender silver wires cunningly inlaid into the polished wood.

Balancing this venerable repository, on the left side of the platform, a block of golden marble rose altarlike; and all around this plinth were carven cryptic sigils in the old Zamorian script. Upon this splendid base rested a bowl of chalcedony; and in the translucent basin danced an eternal flame, connected, Conan knew not how, with the worship of the spider-god.

In the center of the raised enclosure, the far end of which was cloaked in a blood-red arras, towered the statue of Zath; behind it, in the far left corner, the wall of the sacred area was recessed. The idol, graven of black onyx, was wrought with such fidelity to nature that Conan was half tempted to believe that the statue could indeed possess the power of life at night. The heavy ovoid body, supported by some sort of frame or table draped in crimson velvet to match the incarnadined wall behind it, seemed in the flickering light to stand without support, while each of the spider's eight jointed limbs, stouter than a galley's oar, rested on the marble pave. The statue reminded Conan unpleasantly of the giant spider he had fought in the Elephant Tower several years before, save that the arachnid here depicted was more than twice the size of that remembered monster.

Across the front of the creature's head—or what would have been its head if members of the spider tribe had possessed heads distinct from the forward segment of their bodies—a row of four great eyes gleamed with a bluish radiance in the lamplight. From where he stood, Conan could perceive that, in addition, Zath had four additional eyes, one pair on the sides of its body and the other pair on top. The sight stirred Conan's predatory instincts, and he whispered to Lar:

"What are those eyes composed of, boy?"

"Sh!" admonished Lar. "Here come the priests."

The walls of the sacred enclosure were pierced by two doors, one on each side beyond the chest and the altar. A staid procession emerged from the left-hand door: a dozen men in silken turbans and brocaded robes, each carrying a staff with a jewel-encrusted knob of gold or silver. In the lead strode one taller than the rest, a man clad in a flowing white garment and a night-black turban, whose bristling black brows, eagle's beak of a nose, and voluminous white beard endowed him with a formidable air.

Rainbow-hued were the vestments of the other priests. One wore a scarlet gown and azure headgear; another a purple robe topped by a saffron turban; and yet another a gown of sapphire blue surmounted by a headdress of pale celadon. Conan recognized the Vicar, Harpagus, by his sable robe and snowy turban.

The twelve priests formed a line before the spider-god. At a gesture from Harpagus, the congregation raised their arms aloft and cried in unison: "Hail Zath, god of all! Hail Feridun, apostle of Zath!"

Next, led by a young priest whose long, tapering fingers beat rhythmically upon the fetid air, the congregation sang a hymn. Conan comprehended but a few snatches of the paean, but he gathered that the refrain proclaimed Zath's purity, which stretched across Zamora like a vast spiderweb.

Four priests then moved majestically forward to surround the eternal flame. Each produced an object from the flowing sleeves of his garment. Conan glimpsed a silver chalice, a dagger with a jeweled hilt, a bronzen mirror, and a golden key. The priests performed some complex rite, causing the flame to emit a curling column of smoke; they passed the symbolic objects through the billowing curls of the smoke, chanting incantations in words that Conan could not understand.

Then the priests, with measured tread, formed two lines along the side walls of the sanctum, as through the right-hand door eight dancing girls approached the spider-god. All were naked save for enormous strings of jet-black beads, intricately threaded to resemble the webs of spiders. Jewels flashed in their ebon hair and on their graceful fingers like dewdrops in the morning sun.

He who wore the sapphire robe produced a flute and played a haunting melody, to which the girls performed a stately dance around the mammoth idol, their strings of beads jingling and clashing as their slender bodies swayed and undulated. Conan whispered:

"I thought Zath was a god of purity. Those lassies look not to me like a preachment for chastity."

"Sh, sir! You do not understand," breathed the boy, his eyes alight with religious fervor. "This is a sacred dance, ancient and honorable. The virtue of our dancing girls is guarded with the utmost vigilance."

Conan's devil whispered to him that, if such were the case, to carry off one of the maidens as his leman were a boast-worthy feat. He persisted: "Which one is your sister?"

"That one—to the left of the center—now she's gone behind the statue. She is taller than the others."

"A handsome filly," muttered Conan to himself, "if she be the one I think she is." The girl was indeed taller and more voluptuously formed than the majority of the small, spare Zamorian women, and Conan felt his blood stir as he watched.

The dance ended with the eight girls prostrating them-selves around the idol, one at the tip of each of the spidery legs. Then, rising and holding hands to form a chain, they filed out of the sanctum, while High Priest Feridun strode forward to rest the knuckles of his left hand upon the lid of the ancient chest. Commanding silence with a raised right hand, he launched into a sermon:

"Dearly beloved: We have expounded before on the sad state into which the once-great nation of Zamora hath fallen. We of the priesthood have expatiated—so far in vain, alas—upon the sins and depravity of the people. Corruption spreadeth amongst you, its source being the throne of your kings, and daily transformeth our once-proud nation into a cauldron of crime, intrigue, and other wickedness. All about us theft, murder, bribery, drunkenness, and fornication pre-vail. The cults of the other gods, which claim to combat this degeneracy, have either failed in their duty or—woe unto Zamora!—have joined in the scramble for illicit wealth and condoned men's wallowing in sensual pleasure."

The old priest's hortatory tones irritated Conan, arousing

in him a perverse desire to cry out that, while the folk of
Zamora were surely wicked enough, they were not so much
worse than those of other nations. But aware that one man
cannot fight hundreds inflamed with religious fanaticism,
he held his tongue. High Priest Feridun continued:

"Only the True Faith of Zath hath retained its integrity of
motive and of practice. Only the True Faith of Zath can
purify the realm and restore Zamora to its ancient greatness.
We do assure you, dearly beloved, that the day of cleansing
draweth nigh. All of you standing devoutly here shall live to
witness it. There shall be a great overturn, a destruction of
the wicked, the like of which the world hath never witnessed; but ye shall see it. The flame of the great purifica-
tion shall sweep across the land, consuming the sinful like
insects dropped into a roaring fire! It cometh apace! Hold
yourselves ready, dear ones, to serve as soldiers in the holy
army of Zath . . . ."

As Feridun continued in this vein, Conan fidgeted with
impatience, until at last the High Priest terminated his ora-
tory with a chanted prayer. Then the eight girls, now clad in
voluminous, if gauzy, robes of rainbow hues, filed solemnly
out and sang a hymn to the wail of the flute in the hands of
him who wore the sapphire robe and celadon turban. Meanwhile, acolytes in emerald tunics circulated among the congregation, shaking their offering bowls. The tinkle of coins
furnished a cheerful if irregular accompaniment to the high-
pitched chorus of maidens.

One acolyte thrust a bowl at Conan. Peering into its
depths, the Cimmerian perceived a heap of coins of various
denominations. Grumbling, he dug a small copper out of his
well-worn purse and dropped it on the heap.

The acolyte sniffed disdainfully. "You are not over-gener-
ous to the god, stranger," he murmured.

"Let the priests increase the sum they pay me as smith,"
growled Conan, "and I'll give you more." The acolyte
opened his mouth, as for a sharp reply; but Conan's glower
persuaded him to bite back his words and pass on to gather
the next gratuity.

When the last offerings had been collected, the temple
maidens ended their song and disappeared. High Priest
Feridun stepped to the chest, ceremoniously unlocked it,
and raised the lid. The acolytes paraded past, each emptying

his bowl of coins, and the ringing clash of their falling echoed from the temple's gilded dome.

Feridun intoned another prayer, blessing the offerings, and re-locked the replenished coffer. Again the congregation lifted their voices in song; Zath was once more hailed with upraised arms, and the service came to its end.

As Conan and the boy left the temple enclosure, Lar, bubbling with youthful enthusiasm, ventured: "Isn't High Priest Feridun a wonderful man? Does he not fill your heart with spiritual inspiration?"

Conan paused before answering. "I have not found priests much different from other men. All work for their own wealth, power, and glory, like the rest of us, however much they mask ambition by pious chatter."

"Oh, sir!" ejaculated the boy. "Let not such impious sentiments come to the ears of the priests of Zath! True, they might excuse you as naught but an ignorant foreigner; but you should never speak lightly of the god and his ministers in holy Yezud—not, that is, unless you would fain serve as fodder for the spider-god."

"Is that the fate of malefactors here?" queried Conan.

"Aye, sir. It is our regular form of execution."

"How is it done?"

"The acolytes throw the criminal into the tunnels beneath the temple. Then, when immortal Zath takes on his mortal form at night, he descends thither to devour the miscreant."

"Who has seen Zath thus scuttling about?"

"Only the priests, sir."

"Has any plain citizen of Yezud witnessed this miracle?"

"N-no, sir. None dares enter the haunts of the spider-god, save the highest ranks of the priesthood. I did hear a tale last year, that one impious wight secretly entered the tunnels, hoping to find valuables to steal. You know what they say about Zamorian thieves?"

"That they are the most skillful in the world and the most faithful to their trust. What befell this venturesome fellow? Did Zath devour him?"

"Nay; he escaped." The boy shuddered. "But he came out raving mad and died a few days thereafter."

"Hm. No place to tarry for one's health, meseems. Tell

me, Lar, of what substance are the eyes of Zath composed?"

"Why, of the same stuff as yours and mine, I suppose; save that when Zath returns to his pedestal and settles into his stony form, his eyes must become some sort of bluish mineral. More I cannot tell."

Conan walked in silence to Lar's home for the midday meal, his nimble mind already scheming. The eyes of Zath were certainly gems of some kind. If he could manage to steal some of them, he would command enough wealth for a lifetime. Usually Conan trod lightly in the presence of strange gods; but he found it difficult to attribute divinity to any spider, however formidable. Whether or not the statue possessed the power to transform itself into a sentient being, Conan could not bring himself to accord it godhood. He felt sure that the priests of Zath were swindling the credulous Zamorians, and that it would be simple justice for him to deprive them of part of their ill-gotten gains.

After the evening repast, Conan, weary of the sobriety of Yezud, strapped on his sword and strode down the rocky ramp to Bartakes's Inn in Khesron. He was pleased to find few other patrons in the common room, for he wished to be alone to think.

Conan carried his jack of wine from the innkeeper's counter and settled down in a corner. He regretted having spoken so cynically to young Lar about gods and priests because, he realized, his incautious words had given the pious and impressionable boy a hold upon him. If they should ever quarrel, or if Lar did something stupid and Conan cuffed him for it, Lar might run to the priests with an exaggerated tale of the blacksmith's heresies. Of the many hard lessons he was being forced to learn in order to make his way in civilized lands, Conan found guarding his tongue and weighing his words the hardest.

The Cimmerian's dour musings were interrupted by the crackle of sharp words across the dim-lit room, where a man and a woman sat with an empty bottle of wine between them. The woman, clad in a tight dress of red and white checked cotton, cut to display a generous expanse of bosom, Conan recognized as Bartakes's daughter Mandana. The man—Conan tensed, for he should have recognized the bristling red mustache immediately upon entering the common room—was Captain Catigern. Preoccupied with his own thoughts, Conan had overlooked the mercenary officer.

Catigern had obviously drunk more than he could handle, and the woman was berating him for his sodden condition. In the midst of her scolding, he made a rude noise, laid his head on his forearms and went to sleep.

The woman pushed back her stool and, glancing boldly around the room, strolled over to Conan's table, saying: "May I join you, Master Nial?"

"Certes," said Conan. "What's your trouble, lass?"

"You can see for yourself." She jerked a thumb toward the somnolent Catigern. "He promised me a glorious evening, and what does he do but drink himself into a brutish stupor! I am sure that you, at least, would not fall asleep when came the time to pleasure your woman." She smiled provocatively and settled the bodice of her dress until her bulging breasts almost burst from their scanty covering.

Conan raised his heavy eyebrows. "Oho!" he murmured in a voice thickening with desire. "If that be the pleasure you require, I'm your man! Just name the time and place."

"Shortly, in my chambers upstairs. But let us drink a little first; and then you must pay my father's tariff for my affections." With a nod of her head she indicated the counter, behind which Bartakes stood.

Conan's eyes grew wary. "How much does he demand?"

"Ten coppers. By the bye, you returned not to the inn after your first night here; did you then gain employment with the priests of Yezud?"

"Aye; I'm now the temple's blacksmith," answered Conan, digging into his purse and counting out coins. "As peaceful trades go, it is not bad—"

Conan left his sentence hanging. Captain Catigern had awakened, lurched to his feet, and now towered above the table at which Conan and Mandana sat. He roared:

"What are you doing with my girl, you oaf?"

Conan studied the speaker with narrowed eyes, gauging the degree of the captain's insobriety. "You can go to hell, Captain," he said evenly. "The wench sought me out of her own free will, whilst you lay snoring in a stupor." He picked up his mug and took a lingering sip.

"Insolent puppy!" shouted Catigern, aiming a back-handed blow at Conan's face. The knuckles of the Brythunian's open hand struck Conan's upraised forearm, splashing his wine. With deliberation, Conan set down the mug, rose as lithely as a jungle cat, and shot his left fist into Catigern's face. The captain's head snapped back; he staggered and fell heavily. The blow would have deprived an ordinary man of consciousness, if it did not do him more substantial damage; but Catigern was an unusually large and powerful man. Hence he was up again in an instant, lugging out his sword.

"I'll carve out your liver and feed it to my dogs!" he snarled, rushing at Conan.

Ignoring a shouted plea from the taverner, Conan met Catigern halfway with his drawn Turanian scimitar, and their clanging blades flashed in the yellow lamplight. Several patrons ducked beneath their tables as the two large men circled, slashing and parrying. The ring of steel upon steel, mingled with the shouts of excited spectators, echoed like a demoniac uproar upon the evening air.

After the first whirlwind exchange of cuts and parries, when Captain Catigern had begun to pant for breath, he changed his tactics. His sword, like most of those used in the West, was straight, whereas Conan's scimitar, heavier than most Turanian blades, was curved like a crescent moon, and therefore useless for thrusting. Now the Brythunian, instead of trading cuts, began to aim swift, deadly thrusts between his hasty parries.

While Conan had ofttimes handled Western swords before coming to Turan, for the past two years all his training and practice had been with the curving saber. Thrice, only his pantherlike agility, combined with desperate parries, saved him from being spitted on Catigern's fine-honed blade. One thrust, like the strike of a serpent, ripped Conan's tunic and scored a bloody scratch across his shoulder.

The Brythunian, he realized, was an experienced fighter, not easily worsted even when rendered unsteady by drink. Although Conan was taller, stronger, faster, and younger, he deemed it fortunate that the skillful mercenary was not quite sober.

Bartakes danced about the combatants in an agony of apprehension, wringing his pudgy hands and crying: "Outside, I pray, gentlemen! Do not fight within my premises! You will bring ruin upon me!"

The duellists ignored him. Then from a dark corner of the common room, a small, shadowy figure glided toward Catigern's back; and Conan caught the gleam of a dagger in the lamplight.

While Conan would willingly kill his adversary in a fair fight, a stab in the back of a man who faced another foe affronted his code of honor. Yet if Conan cried a warning of the danger, the Brythunian would think it merely a cunning distraction so that his antagonist could sword him with impunity.

All this flashed through Conan's mind in less time than it took him to swing his curved sword. With the lightning speed of a leaping leopard, he bounded backward, at the same time grounding the point of his scimitar.

"Behind you!" he bellowed. "Treachery!"

Finding himself momentarily beyond Conan's reach, Catigern whirled to glance behind him. As he whipped around, the unknown assassin threw up his dagger arm to drive a long poniard into the Brythunian's body. With a furious curse, Catigern sent a terrific backhand slash into the assassin's side. The blade sank in between the man's ribs and pelvis, almost severing his spine. The impact hurled the slender man against a trestle table, to strike the floor in a welter of blood and entrails. He moaned briefly and lay still.

"A mighty stroke," commented Conan, his point still fixed upon the floor. "Do you want to fight some more?"

"If you two great idiots—" began Bartakes, but his words were lost on the steely-eyed twain.

"Nay, nay," replied Catigern. He wiped his blade on a corner of the dead man's tunic and started to sheathe it, pausing only to assure himself that Conan was doing likewise. "I cannot kill a man who has just saved my life, even if he tried to slay me but a moment earlier. As to the girl—why, where the devil is the chit?"

Bartakes said: "Whilst you two were fighting, she slipped away to her chamber with another patron—one of your company, I believe, Captain." The innkeeper turned to shout for his sons to remove the body and scrub the floor boards clean. Then, shaking his head, he muttered: "Zath save me from another such pair of young fools!"

Catigern gave a wry smile. "You are right, my friend; we

were fools, sure enough, to risk our lives over a public woman." He yawned. "As for me—"

"Wait," growled Conan. "Let's see who wanted to stick a knife into you. Fetch one of those lamps, innkeeper."

Turning over the mangled body, Conan saw that the man was a typical Zamorian, small, slight, and dark. Conan asked: "Know you this man, Bartakes?"

"Surely!" replied the taverner. "He rode in on a mule only today and took a bed, giving his name as Varathran of Shadizar."

"Had you ever clapped eyes upon him ere today?"

"Never. But folk from every corner of Zamora come here to do honor to the spider-god."

Conan ran practiced hands over the corpse. Suspended from Varathran's belt he found a wallet, containing a handful of silver and copper coinage and a small roll of parchment. Conan unrolled the parchment and frowned over it. At last he said:

"Catigern, do you read Zamorian?"

"Not I! I can scarcely read the writing of my native land. What of you?"

"I once learned a few Zamorian characters, but I've forgotten what little I once knew."

"Let me see that," said the innkeeper. Holding the parchment close to the lamp and silently moving his lips, he pored over the spidery script. At last, with a shrug of despair, he returned the roll to Conan.

"It's penned in Old Zamorian," he said, "a script gone clean out of use since Mithridates the First revised our system of writing. Perchance a priest in Yezud could decipher it; I cannot."

"May I see it?" purred a soft, high-pitched voice with a peculiar accent. The Stygian, whom Conan had earlier beheld seated among his scrolls and tablets, now stood expectantly at his shoulder. "I may be of some assistance to you, sir."

Conan frowned. "And who might you be?"

The shaven-headed one smiled. "I am called Psamitek of Luxur, a poor student of arcane arts."

With a grunt, Conan handed over the scroll, and the Stygian studied it in the flickering lamplight. "Let me see: 'I— Tughril—High Priest—of Erlik—do hereby swear—by my god—to pay—ten thousand—pieces of gold—for the head—what is this name? C-co—nan—the Cimmerian.' What make you of it, sirs? Who is this Conan? Is any here so named?"

Catigern cast a fleet glance about the room; then he and Conan shook their heads. Bartakes spoke: "I mind me that two years agone, when I visited Shadizar, I heard of a notorious thief, hight Conan. I had forgotten the story until yon parchment named him. 'Twas said the fellow's depredations were so outrageous that every guard and watchman in Zamora was sworn to seek him out. At last he fled the country and disappeared."

The Stygian murmured: "So? I doubt not there is some connection, however mysterious it seem. This Conan's head must have some singular quality, that a Turanian priest should offer a royal ransom for it. With such a sum, one could accumulate the greatest library of occult works in all of Stygia." With a sigh, he rolled up the parchment and slipped it into his pouch. "Since the message does not concern those present, none will object to my keeping this sheet, I am sure. Good parchment is costly, and this I can pumice off and use again. A good night to you all."

The Stygian bowed obsequiously and withdrew. Conan opened his mouth to demand the return of the scroll; but realizing that he could not make an issue of the matter without exposing his true identity, he ground his teeth in silent vexation. To cover his discomfiture, he turned to Catigern. "Captain, let's have a drink together while our host cleans up. Methinks we've earned it, and what better way to spend this little treasure trove?"

"Good!" said Catigern. "Tomorrow I shall have to report this slaying to the Vicar. You may be called in to testify on my account."

"Is not civilization hell?" grunted Conan. "You cannot even kill a man in honest self-defense without accounting for it to some damned nosy official!"

Later that night, the men of the Free Company on guard duty at the gates of Yezud were startled to see, by starlight, their captain and the town blacksmith, with arms around each other's necks, staggering up the cliffside path. They were singing in powerful bass voices—singing not one song but two.

VII. Wine of Kyros

Three days later, when Conan accompanied Lar to Amytis's house for supper, he found Rudabeh there. Lar said:

"Hail, sister! This is our new blacksmith, the mighty Master Nial. He lets me hold the workpiece on the anvil, to get the feel of the tools, whilst he smites the iron. And today he explained the color changes in the metal as it heats and cools. I shall be a smith yet."

"That is good of you, Master Nial," said Rudabeh with a radiant smile.

Conan's eyes burned a volcanic blue as he looked at the girl. She was tall for a Zamorian and handsome—not the sort of fabulous beauty that kings chose for their seraglios, but clean, healthy, and regular-featured. Nor did the plain tunic and baggy pantaloons of the Zamorian woman's street attire entirely mask her supple, well-rounded dancer's body. She continued:

"Mother has repeated to me some of the tales of high adventure wherewith you have regaled my family. Are they indeed all true?"

"Close enough," grinned Conan, "albeit a good story-teller must stretch a few details for the sake of his art. Did I not see you dance before Zath at the last service in the temple?"

"If you were amongst the worshipers, you did."

"You look more warmly clad now than you were then, girl."

She smiled, seemingly unperturbed. "That is so. But let not my temple costume stir lascivious thoughts within your bosom. I will not become a feast for Zath to furnish any man with momentary pleasure."

Conan growled: "Anyone who tried to feed you to that overgrown bug would answer to me!"

"Your words are fine and brave, Master Nial, but you could not forestall my fate if the priests decided upon it." She gave a little sigh. "Sometimes methinks the holy fathers carry virtue to the point of vice; but, having chosen my route, I must travel it to the end."

"When does your term of service run out?"

"Eight months hence."

"What will you do then?" asked Conan as Amytis set the fleshpot on the table and the diners began spooning out portions of stew.

"Marry some local lad, I ween. Several have made sheep's eyes at me, but I have given the matter little thought. My temple duties fully occupy my waking hours.

"How do you pass your days?"

"As leader of the troupe, I lead the other girls in the sacred songs and dances and train the novices. When we are neither dancing nor singing, we act as handmaidens to the priests and clean the rooms within the temple.

"But these are not my only duties. The old Master of the Properties has lately died, and they have designated me Mistress of the Properties in his stead. The priests could not agree upon one of their own number for the post, so they pushed the task off on me."

"What does the Mistress of the Properties do?"

"I am responsible for all the surfaces of the temple and all the movables therein. I count and polish ornaments and furniture and sacred vessels and the like, and keep lists. So busy am I that I scarce can visit Mother once a fortnight."

"Do you spend the night at home on such occasions?"

"Nay; I must return to the temple ere midnight."

For a while, Conan ate in silence. When Amytis carried off the plates and sent Lar to the well for a bucket of water to wash them with, Conan said:

"Have you ever been to Bartakes's Inn in Khesron, Rud-abeh?"

"Once, years ago, when Father lived, he took us all there. I do not remember much about it."

"They have a new harper, said to be good. May I escort you thither for the evening? I'll see you get back to the tem-ple in ample time."

She sighed again. "How I should love it! But during my term of temple service, I am forbidden to set foot outside Yezud, unless accompanied by a priest. They would whip me if they caught me out of bounds."

"Oh, come on! Wear a veil or a cloak with a hood, and do not show your face. A girl like you should have some life outside her duties."

"You tempt me, sir; I have seen so little of the outer world. But still . . . ."

In low voices, they argued back and forth. Eventually Rudabeh gave in. "Wait here but a moment," she said.

When she reappeared, she was bundled up to the eyes. "Crom!" exclaimed Conan. "You look like one of the mum-mies of Stygia they tell about. Well, come along; the night grows no younger."

The common room of Bartakes's Inn throbbed with the sound of many voices. Conan's fierce blue eyes roved among the tables, seeking the face of anyone who might cause trou-ble for the girl or for himself, before he led the heavily veiled Rudabeh to a dark corner and seated her.

The Stygian scholar sat by himself, studying scrolls and tablets as before. A party of new arrivals occupied an adja-cent table—four men in Hyrkanian traveling dress, their trews tucked into heavy boots, their sheepskin caps, with upturned brims, perched at jaunty angles on their shaven skulls. They were noisily throwing dice as they quaffed great jacks of ale.

Probably Turanians, thought Conan; certainly the fifth newcomer, seated at a small table by himself, was from Turan. Of all the branches of the Hyrkanian race, the Turani-ans, deeming themselves the most civilized, scorned their nomadic kinsmen, who roamed the boundless steppes east of the Vilayet Sea. Yet these same Turanians retained the

physical features and many of the customs and attitudes of
their barbaric forebears and present kinsmen.

The solitary Turanian, hunched over several sheets of
parchment, was short and squarely built, with a neatly-
trimmed gray beard. Much finer than the clothing of the
other four was his attire; and an embroidered black velvet
skullcap, richly strewn with luminescent pearls, rested on
his close-cut graying hair. He had pushed aside the platter
with the cold remains of his dinner to make room for the
documents on which he focused his attention.

Conan had a lingering impression that he had seen the
man before, but he could not recall the circumstances. At
least, he was sure it was not in Yezud, so he dismissed the
matter from his mind. He snapped his fingers to summon
Bartakes's daughter Mandana, who at the moment manned
the wine counter. Keeping his voice low, he murmured:

"Wine for the lady and me—a fine wine, none of your
ordinary slop. What have you?"

Mandana shot a hostile glance at the veiled figure and
answered: "We have Numalian red, and Ianthic red, and
white of Akkharia."

"Are those the choicest in the house?"

Mandana gave a disdainful little sniff. "'Tis true we have
a cask of the white of Kyros, but that is for high-born ladies
and gentlemen. *You* could never afford—"

"The contents of my purse are no concern of yours!"
growled Conan, slapping down a handful of silver. "Bring
out the best."

Mandana flounced off. For the moment, Conan enjoyed
an unaccustomed prosperity, for he had made a discovery
about his present situation. During the illness of Pariskas,
smithery work had so piled up that Conan's patrons, eager to
obtain their work out of its proper turn, thrust upon him siz-
able sums, over and above the stipend paid him by the
temple.

Soon two goblets of golden Kyrian appeared on his table.
Instead of draining his goblet in three gulps, as was his usual
wont, Conan endeavored to pursue the civilized custom of
sniffing the aroma and delicately savoring each sip. Consid-
ering the cost of the beverage, even Conan, careless though
he was with money, wanted to make each drink last a while.

"This wine is wonderful!" whispered Rudabeh, who had partly raised her veil. "I have never tasted aught like it in my life."

"I thought you might enjoy it," said Conan expansively. "How go the intrigues at the te—at your place of employment?"

"Something is brewing," she replied thoughtfully, barely above a whisper. "When my master talks of cleansing the kingdom, he is not merely casting words upon the wind. He has some terrible plan in mind and hints that he will shortly act—perhaps within a month."

Conan leaned forward to murmur: "What sort of wight is the High Priest?"

Rudabeh shuddered delicately. "We all fear him," she breathed. "He is a stern, unbending taskmaster—just according to his reckoning, but without mercy when he deems himself in the right, and he always thinks himself in the right."

Conan looked at Rudabeh through narrowed eyes, his heavy brows drawn in concentration. "What action does he plan?"

"I know not. And then there is this visit by—" She nodded toward the tables whereat lounged the four in sheepskin caps and the lone gray-bearded scholar in the pearl-spangled cap.

"What do you know of those fellows?" asked Conan.

"They come from Aghrapur, sent by King Yildiz on some mission to the temple. I do not know the names of those four ruffians; but the older man is Lord Parvez, a Turanian diplomat."

Conan clapped a large, muscular hand against his forehead. "Of course! I—" He checked himself in time to avoid blurting out that he had seen Parvez at Yildiz's court, a place where—according to his present story, he had never set foot. To cover his confusion, he signaled Mandana to refill their goblets. Rudabeh, noting Conan's discomfiture, whispered:

"Why, know you this Parvez?"

"Nay, I did but hear of him in Shadizar," muttered Conan lamely. "What can he want with Feridun? Kings send ambassadors to other kings, not to the priests of foreign lands."

"Again, I know not; but it might have some connection with the veiled woman."

"Veiled woman? What veiled woman?" asked Conan sharply. An idea was forming in his agile mind, just beyond the bounds of consciousness.

"Ere you came to Yezud, the Vicar returned from a lengthy journey, bringing with him a woman swathed in many-colored veils. He hustled her into the temple, where she remains in a locked chamber, seen by none save the priests of the highest rank and a single slave. This servant, a swarthy wench, comes from some far country and speaks no tongue I know."

Like a meteor, the idea burst upon Conan's consciousness: the woman must be the princess Jamilah, favorite wife of King Yildiz. He pressed his lips together lest he divulge his knowledge of Jamilah's abduction. Trying to seem casual, he said: "This woman, now—might your priests have kidnapped her for ransom?"

Rudabeh shook her head. "Nay; Zath and those who serve him are enormously rich. The coins in the offering chest are but a token of the temple's wealth. The real treasures of Zath—the vessels of gold and silver, set with diamonds and emeralds and rubies; the stacks of bars of precious metal; the heaps of uncut gems—are held in triple-locked and guarded crypts. Besides the tithes of the faithful and the gifts of the king, the temple controls the traffic in bitumen, which bubbles from the ground hereabouts and lies in pools until the folk, under the watchful eyes of the priests, scoop it up to sell. Such are the riches of Zath that not even a king's ransom would tempt them to such an outrage. Perchance the woman is some well-born fugitive, who has fled a brutal husband."

"Or poisoned him and now seeks sanctuary," added Conan.

Although Rudabeh's words gave Conan material for furious thought and set his eyes agleam with avarice, he dared not pursue the subject of the temple's wealth and the sequestered queen lest he arouse suspicion in the mind of his companion or of the company around them. To mask his thoughts, he affected a careless smile, drained his goblet of wine, and signaled Mandana to refill the tumblers. When the sullen girl had fulfilled her task, she stared insolently at Rudabeh before withdrawing. The dancer drew down her half-raised veil and shrank back into the corner. Conan said:

"Pay the wench no heed. Her nose is out of joint with envy of your handsome cloak, no more. Now tell me how you spend the hours of your day."

Rudabeh, he found, was a lively talker: intelligent, clear-sighted, and not without wit. The women he had known since leaving Cimmeria had all chattered foolishly, regarding talk only as a preliminary to lovemaking, or to refusal, as the case might be. He enjoyed Rudabeh's talk for its own sake, and the contact with her keen mind proved a new and stimulating experience. She told him softly:

"One of my tasks is to keep watch on the reservoir whence feeds the sacred flame."

"How is that done?"

"The flame burns bitumen from a wick of braided fabric, set in oil in a hollow in the block of marble, beneath the chalcedony bowl. In the recess by the door whence the priests enter the naos for services, a pipe juts out, to which a bronzen valve is affixed. I turn the valve to the left, and oil flows; to the right, and the flow ceases."

"An ingenious device," mused Conan. "I have seen royal palaces that had been better off for such amenities. How is the reservoir filled?"

"Every day," she continued, "I must needs inspect the reservoir to see how low the oil has sunk. When it is low—say, after three days—I inform the priest whose duty it is. He fills a pitcher at the pipe and pours the bitumen into the reservoir.

"Last year, saying they had more work than they could accomplish, the priests appointed me to perform that task. But the first time I tried it, being new to the job, I spilled some bitumen, and the High Priest was furious. You'd have thought I had stolen one of the Eyes of Zath. Later he blamed me when the priest Mirzes set fire to his robe, claiming I had not cleaned up the oil sufficiently so that Mirzes slipped on the marble."

"How could that start a fire?" asked Conan.

"Mirzes got careless during the Presentation of the Telesms—when they bring out the sacred key and mirror and so on—and waved his arm across the eternal flame. His fluttery sleeve caught fire, and there was much dashing about and shouting ere they beat the fire out."

"What was the upshot?"

"Mirzes had his arm in bandages for a fortnight. As soon as he was well, the High Priest gave him the task of filling the reservoir, saying that he, if anyone, would appreciate the need for care. I did not mind escaping that chore, albeit I resented Feridun's barbed comments on the stupidity of women."

"Whence comes this oil?"

"I know not for certain, but one told me the pipe lies beneath the ground outside the temple and leads up to a gorge, wherein the bitumen seeps from the soil and forms a pool."

Conan nodded his understanding. "And speaking of the Eyes of Zath, they must be gems of some sort—at least when Zath is in his stony form. Do you know what sort?"

"'Tis said they are eight matchless specimens of the Kambujan girasol, or as some say, fire opal. Their value must be as great as all the rest of the treasure of Zath." Glancing around, Rudabeh suddenly stiffened and caught Conan's hand in a convulsive grip. "Nial! We must flee!"

"Why? What's up, lass?"

"See you that man who just entered?" She moved her head slightly to indicate direction. "Nay, do not stare; but that man is Darius, one of the priests! If he sees me, I am undone!"

The individual indicated was one of the younger priests, a slim, ascetic-looking man not much older than Conan, clad in an amber robe and an emerald turban. Paying no attention to the other patrons, Darius walked quietly across the floor to where sat the Stygian scholar. The two greeted each other with bows and stately gestures before the priest pulled up a stool and sat facing Psamitek. The priest and the Stygian spoke in low voices, while Psamitek made notes on a waxed wooden tablet.

"I've heard of this Stygian," murmured Rudabeh. "He travels about, studying the cults of many gods; and now he wishes instruction in the theology of Zathism. I suppose Darius is imparting it to him. Now shall we go?"

Conan shook his head slightly. "We must not leap up and depart in haste, for that would draw attention. Besides, he seems completely absorbed in what he's telling the Stygian."

"At least," breathed Rudabeh, "Darius is one of whom I have little fear. He is unworldly and idealistic, and gossip says he is at outs with the High Priest and the Vicar. Behold, here comes the harper. Dare we wait to hear him?"

"Surely!" said Conan. "I'll order one more cup for each of us ere he begins." He waved to Mandana.

Rudabeh yawned, then smiled through her veil. "I ought not to drink so much, but this wine is so refreshing. What is it called?"

"Wine of Kyros, from the coast of Shem. I hear the combination of climate and soil makes it the world's best; and if there be a better, I have yet to taste it."

The harper sat on his stool and tuned his instrument. Sweeping skilled hands across the strings, he sang a tragic lament in a voice quivering with despair. At the end he got a brief round of applause. He acknowledged it with a bow, then passed around the room, holding out his cap for donations.

His next song was a rollicking ballad about a fabled robber who stole from the rich but gave to the poor. But now a dispute broke out among the four Turanians, whose angry voices nearly drowned out the delicate chords of the harp and the fluting voice of the singer. Several patrons tried to quiet them, but they paid no heed. Since they were speaking Hyrkanian, Conan could follow the thrust of the dispute.

The Turanians were arguing over who should enjoy the favors of Mandana for the night. Conan had been discomfited to learn that Bartakes rented out his daughter for this purpose. Although he had shed most of the stern moral code of his barbaric homeland, Conan considered it dishonorable for any man to prostitute his kinswoman. But then, he told himself, what could one expect of decadent Zamorians? Besides, he admitted, before he met Rudabeh he had intended to avail himself of the tavern wench's services.

The dispute was at length referred to the dice box, and for a while the twang of the harp competed with the rattle of dice. Then a shout announced the winner, and the other three congratulated him with loud, lewd jests.

Rudabeh, taking a sip of her wine, said: "It is—it is a shame we cannot hear the music. Nial, can naught be done to quiet those louts?"

Conan had resolved not to let himself be drawn into any brawls that night. He feared that either his identity or that of his companion might be exposed, or that—if nothing worse—Bartakes would forbid him the premises. On the other hand, it went against his nature to sit supinely by while a woman in distress appealed to him for aid.

Before he could decide which impulse to follow, one of the Turanians rose unsteadily to his feet and lurched across the common room to Conan's table. He slapped Conan on the shoulders and barked in broken Zamorian:

"You, fellow! How much you take for loan of your woman for this night?"

Keeping a tight rein on his volcanic temper, Conan replied: "My woman, as you call her, is not for sale or rent. Besides, I thought you had already gained the innkeeper's daughter?"

Swaying, the Turanian spat on the floor. "That was Tutush won her, not me. Here I am, randy as goat and no woman. What you take? I pay good money."

"I have told you," grated Conan, "the lady is not for sale."

The Turanian gave Conan a cuff on the shoulder that was somewhere between a friendly pat and a hostile blow. "Oh, do not play great lord with me! I Chagor, mighty swordsman. When I want, by Erlik I take—"

Conan snapped to his feet and brought his fist up in a whistling arc to Chagor's jaw. The fist connected with a jarring smack, and the Turanian fell backwards as if poleaxed. His face expressionless, Conan sat down and took a swallow of wine.

But the Turanian's facilities soon returned to him. He reached out feebly, trying to regain his feet. Conan rose again, turned Chagor over with his boot, and grasped him by the slack of his jacket and trews. Carrying the man to the door, he kicked it open, strode out, and dropped the Turanian into the horse trough. After pulling him out of the water and dipping him back several times, he dropped him in the dirt and reëntered the inn.

Scarcely had the door closed when he found himself facing Chagor's three companions, each with scimitar bared. With the quickness of a pouncing panther, Conan swept out his own blade. He was about to launch a headlong attack, knowing that only by tigerish speed could he hope to keep his three adversaries from surrounding him and cutting him down. Then from behind the Turanians, a voice commanded in Hyrkanian:

"Hold! Put up your swords! Back to your table, clods!"

The graybeard with the skullcap had risen to thunder his orders in a voice like the crack of a whip. To Conan's astonishment, the lumbering Turanians obeyed promptly. They backed away, sheathed their sabers, and returned, sullen and grumbling, to their table.

Conan scabbarded his own sword and strode back to his table. There he found that Rudabeh, sitting with her back to the corner, had dozed off and slept through the noisy confrontation.

The harper had disappeared. The young priest who had been in conversation with the Stygian scholar rose, nodded to his acquaintance, and hurried out.

Conan took a draft of wine and looked up to see Parvez standing by his table. The diplomat said: "Good even, Captain Conan! And how are things in Yezud?"

Conan growled: "I thank you for stopping the brawl, sir, but I am Nial the blacksmith."

With a chuckle, the Turanian pulled up a vacant stool and sat down. "So that is what you go by here, eh? Very well, you shall be Nial to me. But think not that I do not know you. By the way, what did you with Chagor?"

"I gave him a much-needed bath; you could smell him half a league up-wind. Here he comes now."

Chagor had staggered in dripping. He glared about the room; but when Parvez pointed a stern finger, he went meekly back to the table whereat sat the other three.

"At least, I am glad you did him no lasting harm," said Parvez. "They are good enough fellows, but betimes the devil gets into them."

Conan pushed Rudabeh's goblet toward Parvez. "You may as well finish this, since my companion sleeps."

Parvez sniffed and tasted. "Kyrian, eh? You must be in funds."

"What are you doing here?" countered Conan.

"Diplomatic business." Parvez lowered his voice and glanced around. "Perchance we can be of service to each other. I will tell you a thing or two, since I think I can trust you further than most of the wights hereabouts. I have a hold on you, and I know more about you than you suspect; so it behooves us to put some faith in each other. In Aghrapur you had the name of a man of his word, despite your proclivity for violence."

Tensely, Conan growled: "I'll keep your secrets exactly as well as you keep mine."

"We agree, then? What know you of the abduction of Princess Jamilah?"

Conan told Parvez of his encounter with Harpagus in the Marshes of Mehar. Then he repeated what Rudabeh had told him of the veiled woman. The Cimmerian ended by saying: "How did you trace the lady hither?"

"That required no skill. The High Priest of Zath sent a message to His Majesty, stating that Her Royal Highness was safe and well and would be detained until Feridun's plans had attained fruition."

"But what in the nine hells," asked Conan, "does the temple of Zath want with the princess? They already have all the wealth any mortals could desire. Would they force the worship of Zath upon the kingdom of Turan?"

"Nay—at least not for the nonce. I visited the High Priest this day for the answer to that very question. Feridun scornfully rejected any talk of ransom; and in the course of our speech he revealed more by his omissions than by his admissions. When I put his hints and blusters together, I was convinced that he plans to launch some sort of revolution in Zamora, to cast down the sovereign he terms 'corrupt and effete'. Apparently he seized the princess to make certain that King Yildiz shall not intervene to save his brother monarch, as called for by an ancient treaty. He assured me that the lady will be well cared for until his great 'cleansing' is accomplished."

"I had naught to do with that abduction, as some may think," said Conan gruffly. "I do not use women as counters in a game."

Lord Parvez raised quizzical eyebrows. "I myself first thought that you had helped to carry off the lady, because of your simultaneous disappearance; and it was I who sent forth a warrant for your capture. It was fortunate that you made your escape, for now I think you innocent of that offense, although you remain in bad odor in Turan because of Orkhan's slaying."

"I killed in self-defense," growled Conan, "whatever that bitch Narkia has averred."

Parvez shrugged. "That concerns me not, whatever be the truth of it. High Priest Tughril swears to have your heart for the death of his son, but that is his affair, and yours." Parvez rubbed his chin thoughtfully.

"I know about that, too," said Conan, telling of the assassin Varathran's attack on Catigern and the price that had been placed on Conan's head.

"I don't understand," Conan continued, "why this scum should attack the Brythunian instead of me. We look not alike."

"I can imagine it," said Parvez. "Suppose Tughril sends a man to recruit a trusty murderer. In the gutters of Shadizar, his messenger finds Varathran and tells him: 'Go slay Conan the Cimmerian, a great hulking fellow who has fled to Yezud, to seek service in the temple guard.' With no further description to go by, Varathran arrives here and discovers two great, hulking men enmeshed in battle. One is a palpable civilian, whilst the other wears the habiliments of a captain of mercenaries. Naturally, he takes Catigern for his quarry."

"You seem to have followed my every move hither," said Conan uncomfortably.

"Gathering information is my trade, just as fighting is yours. And now, friend—ah—Nial, I have a proposal to make."

"Well?" growled Conan, his blue eyes lighting with interest.

"I want Jamilah, unharmed. You are the one man whom I count upon to get her."

Conan pondered, then said: "How am I supposed to do that? The lady is hidden in that maze of corridors within the temple, just where I know not. Even if I could locate her, how could I smuggle her past the Brythunian guards? There must be at least a score of those fellows on duty there, day and night."

Parvez waved a negligent hand. "In your former and less respectable days—and don't think I know not of them, too—you performed feats of stealth, daring, and cunning no whit the less."

"But even then, I never learned the art of picking locks. My fellow th—my associates said my thick fingers were too clumsy to make it worth their while to teach me. So how could I enter her locked chamber? I am no weakling, but those stout oaken doors are beyond my power to burst by main force. I should need an axe, the sound of whose strokes would bring the guards on the run."

The Turanian smiled. "As to that, I can help you. When I came hither, it was with His Majesty's orders to recover the lady, by personally invading the temple if need be, or face loss of my head on my return. To tip the odds further in my favor, he caused the royal sorcerer to present me with this bauble."

Parvez produced a bejeweled silver arrow, as long as a man's finger. "This," he said, "is the Clavis of Gazrik, one of the magical gimcracks in the royal strongbox. With it you can unlock any door. Having no practical experience at burglary, I dreaded this undertaking; but your appearance simplifies my task."

"How does that thing work?" queried Conan.

"Touch the point of the arrow to the lock and say *kapinin achilir genishi!* and the lock will unlock itself. The Clavis will even make a bolt slide back, if it be not too heavy. I can lend you the object until your mission be accomplished.

"Hm. What shall be my price for this work?"

"Let me think," said the Turanian. "I can pay you fifty pieces of gold from what I have with me. I must needs keep enough to assure my return to Turan with the lady."

"Hah!" ejaculated Conan. "For such a risk? Not so, my lord. It would have to be much, much more."

"I could recommend you to high office and an additional emolument when I got home. I have influence, and I am sure I could at least assure you of a senior captainship."

Conan shook his head. "Had this come ere my unfortunate encounter with Tughril's son . . . . But as things stand, Tughril has already set one assassin on my trail, and he is likely to set others. From what I know of his little ways with traps and poisons, in Turan I shouldn't have the chance of a snowball in Kush."

"Well, young man, what *do* you wish that is within my power to grant?"

Conan's eyes blazed bluely across the table. "I'll take your fifty pieces of gold—in advance, mind you—and also that silver arrow, but not as a loan. I'll take it to keep."

Parvez argued briefly against giving up the Clavis of Gazrik; but Conan was firm, and the older man gave in. "It is yours," he said at last. "His Majesty will not be pleased, but gratitude for the return of Jamilah may outweigh his resentment at the loss of the bauble." Parvez handed over the arrow and counted out the gold. "I suspect you have further plans for the use of the device. King Yildiz would pay handsomely for the Eyes of Zath."

He winked at Conan and extended a hand, which the Cimmerian gripped to seal the bargain. With a glance at the still-sleeping Rudabeh, Parvez added: "How will you get your fair companion home? At least, I presume she is fair beneath all those swathings."

Conan reached over and shook the girl. He even slapped her lightly, to no avail. Rudabeh slumbered on.

"I'll carry her," grunted Conan, rising. He gathered the dancing girl in his arms and bade Parvez a curt good-night. As he passed the table at which sat the four Turanians of Parvez's suite, Chagor spat on the floor and muttered something that sounded like a threat. Ignoring it, Conan strode out into the starlit night.

The cooler air outside failed to revive Rudabeh, who was still dead to the world. So Conan marched up the hillside path to the gate of Yezud with the girl in his arms. He endured in silence the gibes of the Brythunian guards who opened the small door in the gate for him. He was confident that they would not carry tales to the priests, because to do so might spoil their own off-duty amusements.

Conan had meant to lead Rudabeh directly to the back door of the temple. But it occurred to him that, if he delivered her in this unconscious state, he might get her into the gods only knew what kind of trouble. The priests might ask Conan awkward questions, too. After a moment's thought, he carried her through his smithy and into his private abode.

Since the night was moonless, Conan's room was pitch dark, save for a few dull red coals in the brazier. Feeling his way, he laid Rudabeh on his pallet and loosed her veils. She stirred but did not awaken.

Conan ignited a splinter from the coals in the brazier and lit a candle. When he brought the light closer to Rudabeh, he saw that she was indeed a beautiful girl. As he looked down upon her, his passions rose. The blood pounded in his temples; he set down the candle and began gently to unfasten the girl's garments.

He untied her cloak and spread it out. He unlaced the flimsy jacket and spread it, baring Rudabeh's firm breasts.

The dim-lit room swam to Conan's gaze as he looked upon his prize. His breath quickened. He started to unfasten his own garments when a thought made him pause.

Conan prided himself upon never having forced or deceived a woman. If one wanted to extend her ultimate hospitality to him, he would quickly accept; but he had never coerced a girl or tried to befool her with false promises. To take advantage of Rudabeh's present condition would offend his code almost as gravely as an outright rape.

Still, his passions were strong. For an instant he stood immobile as a statue while the two opposing urges battled within him.

A fleeting vision of his aged mother, back in her Cimmerian village, tipped the balance. Telling himself that there would be other chances openly to solicit Rudabeh's love, he stooped and was just tying up her jacket when she stirred and opened her eyes.

"What do you?" she mumbled.

"Oh," said Conan. "You're alive, thank Mitra. I was going to listen to your heart to see if it still beat."

"I think you had something else in mind," she said as he helped her up. "*Ulp*—I am going to be sick!"

"Not on the floor! Over here!" he pushed her to the wash-stand and bent her head over the basin.

Half an hour later, just before midnight, Conan delivered Rudabeh, clean and sober, to the back door of the temple, on the north side. "I thank you," she said, "but you should not have been so generous with the wine of Kyros."

"I'll be stingier next time. How can I see you again?"

She sighed. "Ere Feridun became High Priest, you could come to this door and knock four times. Then old Oxyathres would open it, and you could tell him which girl you wished speech with and give him a coin. But Feridun has ended all that. Now you must wait until the priests give me leave to spend an evening at home; and that is something not even the keenest astrologer could predict. We shall have to meet by chance at my mother's house again."

"Would you like another visit to Bartakes's place, when that time comes?"

"Ah, no indeed! I dare not go outside the city wall again; it was godlike luck that the priest Darius failed to mark my presence, and I cannot face such a risk a second time."

She gave him a quick kiss and was gone. Conan walked back to his smithy, scowling and muttering. He wondered: if he had taken advantage of her, would it have left him feeling a bigger fool than he felt now?

VIII. The Eight Eyes of Zath

For several days, Conan labored at his craft. He looked forward to seeing Rudabeh again at her mother's home, but the dancing girl failed to appear.

"The way the priests work the poor lass," said Amytis, "a body never knows when she will get home. She is supposed to have four evenings off each month, but it's a lucky month when she gets three."

Once he had caught up with the backlog of work that had piled up in the smithy before his employment, Conan performed his duties in a more leisurely manner. Every day he took an hour or two off to exercise his horse. Once he stopped at Bartakes's Inn to chat with Parvez, who showed increasing impatience.

"I cannot free the woman until I know where she is kept!" expostulated Conan.

"Then you must redouble your efforts to find out," said Parvez. "Rumor tells me that the doom wherewith the High Priest threatens us may be unleashed within a fortnight."

Conan grunted. "Perhaps you are right. I'll do what I can."

The next day, Conan attended another service in the temple of Zath, partly to keep on the good side of the priests and partly to familiarize himself with the layout. He stood through Feridun's harangue predicting the great, purifying revolution. When the dancing girls came on, he stared eagerly to see Rudabeh. At her appearance, he trembled with desire at the sight of her gyrating in nothing but a sparse cobweb of black beads. He tossed a larger coin than before into the acolytes' offering bowl, to give the impression that he was leaning toward the cult of Zath.

He also stared at the great gems that ornamented the statue of the spider-god—eight great opals, each as large as a child's fist; four in a row across the front, one on each side, and two on top. If he could steal them and get away whole, he could go to some far country, buy an estate and a title of nobility, or a high rank in the army, and be secure for life. Not that he would ever cease wandering in search of adventure and danger; but it would be pleasant to know that he had a secure base to return to, where he could rest and enjoy life between bouts of derring-do. He turned over and discarded one plan after another for getting the jewels into his possession.

After the service, he lingered in the vestibule, pretending to get a stone out of his shoe. When the rest of the congregation had streamed out, instead of following them, he entered the corridor leading off from the vestibule to the right as one entered the temple—the side opposite that into which Morcant had led him on his first arrival. He prowled the hallway, glancing keenly to right and left to orient himself and to find clues as to what lay behind the massive oaken doors.

The corridor made a bend, and as Conan came around the corner he found himself facing one of the Brythunian guards. The man stood at the junction of the corridor with another passage, which led off into semi-darkness to the right. From his knowledge of the temple's exterior, Conan was sure that this passage occupied the first of the four wings on that side.

The immediate problem was to allay the suspicions of the guard. Casually, Conan said: "Hail, Urien! Have you lost your pay gaming again?"

The guardsman frowned. "I hold my own. But what do you here, Nial? A layman like you should be accompanied by a priest or an acolyte."

"I do but work in the temple's interest . . . ." began Conan, but stopped as he saw Urien's eyes look past him. He spun around, to find that Harpagus the Vicar, in black robe and white turban, had come up softly behind him. Conan said:

"It occurred to me, Vicar, that some of the metal furnishings in the temple may need repairs. If I could inspect the place, examining every hinge and fitting, I might save trouble anon."

Harpagus gave a cold little smile. "It is good of you to think of our welfare, Nial. The servants of Zath watch vigilantly for such defects. When they find one, they will inform you in due course. How goes your smithery?"

"Well, I thank you," grumbled Conan. "It keeps me occupied."

"Good! One of your customers complained that your craftsmanship was rough compared with your predecessor's. I explained that you had been soldiering and thus were out of practice. I trust we shall see an improvement."

Conan resisted an impulse to tell the Vicar what the dissatisfied customer could do with the piece Conan had made for him. "I'll do my best, sir. I am now on my way to finish an iron ornament for someone's door."

"One moment, Master Nial. I wish speech with you in my closet; but meanwhile I have a small task to perform. Pray walk with me."

Wondering, Conan followed the priest back to the vestibule and out the front doors of the temple. There Conan found that the worshipers, instead of dispersing to their homes and workshops, were kept on the temple steps by the Brythunian guards, holding pikes parallel to the ground to form a barrier. The reason, Conan saw, was that a flock of sheep was being driven in from the city gate. The animals flowed past the front of the temple and around to the west side, chivvied on their way by two skin-clad shepherds and a dog.

When at last the Brythunians raised their pikes, the Vicar strode around the corner after the sheep, while Conan followed the Vicar. They found the flock huddled near the door at the end of the first wing of the temple they came to on that side. This wing, like its fellow on the opposite side, had a massive door set in its end wall.

The dog raced around the flock, chasing animals back into the mass whenever one started to stray. The shepherds leaned on their crooks and watched. The Vicar pushed through the sheep to the door at the end of the wing. Here he thrust back the massive bolt that secured the door from the outside, unlocked the door with a key, and heaved it open. Stepping back, he waved to indicate that the shepherds should drive their flock in.

With the noisy help of their dog, the shepherds forced the sheep into the opening. When the animals were nearly all inside, the dog behaved strangely, backing away from the opening with its hair bristling and snarling, as if it had encountered a strange and menacing smell. The shepherds drove the remaining beasts into the passage by blows of their crooks.

Harpagus closed the door, locked it, and slammed the big bolt across. He turned, put away his key, and from his robe brought out a small purse, which he handed to the older shepherd. The shepherds bowed, mumbled thanks in their dialect, and walked off with their dog.

"Now, Master Nial," said the Vicar, "we shall repair to my cabinet."

Unable to think of a reason to gainsay the command, Conan followed Harpagus into the chamber where he had received his appointment as blacksmith. Harpagus sat down behind his flat-topped writing table, saying: "Look at me, Nial!"

The priest raised the hand that bore the ring set with the huge gemstone. His piercing eyes caught Conan's and held them as he began to wave the ring-decked fingers back and forth. In a low monotone he intoned:

"You are becoming drowsy—drowsy—drowsy. You are losing your will to think for yourself. You shall tell me, truthfully, all that which I am fain to know . . . ."

The priest's eyes seemed to expand to inhuman size; the room faded away, and Conan stood as in a dense fog, seeing nothing save the priest's huge eyes.

Just in time, Conan recalled the lessons he had received from Kushad, the blind seer of Sultanapur. With a mighty effort, he tore his gaze away and concentrated on his mental picture of the room in which he stood, reciting to himself: "Two threes are six; three threes are nine . . . ."

Little by little the fog cleared, and the Vicar's study swam into view. Conan silently faced the Vicar, who said: "Now tell me Nial, what were you truly doing, loitering in the temple after the service, instead of issuing forth with the others?"

"I had a stone in my shoe, my lord. Then the thought struck me that I could better fulfill my duties as smith to the temple by examining the metalwork in this building for defects."

Harpagus frowned in a puzzled manner and repeated the question, receiving the same reply.

"Are you truly under my influence?" asked the Vicar, "or are you shamming?"

"Ask what you will, sir, and I will answer truly."

"Foolish question," muttered Harpagus. "But let us try another. Tell me of your feelings for and relations with the dancer Rudabeh—everything, even to intimate details."

"Mistress Rudabeh is the daughter of the woman at whose house I take my meals," said Conan. "I once supped with the lass when she visited her home; that is all."

"You have never escorted her out—say, to Bartakes's Inn in Khesron?"

"Nay, sir; she said it were against the temple's rules."

"What did you and she discuss when you met her at her mother's house?"

"We talked of local gossip, and I told of my adventures."

"Have you had carnal knowledge of the wench?"

"Nay, sir; I understand that to be forbidden."

Harpagus sat for a moment, tapping an index finger softly on his desk top. At last he said: "Very well. When I snap my fingers, you shall awaken; but you shall remember none of this discourse. Then you may go."

The priest snapped his fingers. Conan drew a long breath, squared his enormous shoulders, and said: "What did you wish to ask me about, my lord Vicar?"

"Oh, I have forgotten," snapped Harpagus testily. "Go on about your business."

Conan nodded, turned, and started to stride out; but the Vicar called: "Eldoc!"

The Brythunian standing guard before Harpagus' door thrust his head in. "Aye, Vicar?"

"Show Master Nial out. And you, Nial," he added severely, "seem prone to forget that we do not allow laymen to wander the temple unescorted. Do not give me occasion to mention this rule again."

Out in the corridor, Conan wiped his sleeve across his

sweat-beaded brow and ground his teeth in suppressed rage. At least, he hoped that his impersonation of a hypnotic subject had taken in the Vicar.

When Conan reached Amytis's house that day, he again found Rudabeh there before him. Since the time was close to midsummer and the light lingered late, they went out after supper into the garden behind the house. Rudabeh said: "Have a care that you step not on our cabbages!"

When Conan had boasted of his adventures, he asked: "What's this doom the High Priest is ever threatening to loose?"

"I know not," she replied. "The inner circle keep their secrets."

"It sounds like some plague. I've heard of sorcerous pestilences."

She shrugged. "All will become clear in time, I ween."

"Sorcery ofttimes escapes the sorcerer's control," mused Conan. "We might well be among the victims."

"You can always flee."

"But what of you?"

She shrugged again. "I must take my chances. Yezud is my home; I am not a wanderer like you, to whom all places are as one."

"If the plague gets loose in Yezud, you may have no kith or kin left."

"If so," she murmured, "that is my fate."

"Oh, curse your Eastern fatalism! Why not flee with me?"

She gave him a level look. "I wondered how soon you would come to that. Know, Nial, that I am no man's plaything. When my term ends, I will settle down with some likely lad, to keep his house and rear his children."

Conan made a wry face. "It sounds as dull as life in my native village. I could show you some real living."

"Doubtless; but to be the drab of a footloose adventurer is not to my taste."

"How do you know, girl, if you've never tried it?"

"If I found housewifery intolerable, I suppose I could flee with a man like you. But if I went with you, I could never return to Yezud; the priests would feed me to Zath."

Conan threw up his hands. "Mitra save me from intelligent women, who plan their lives like a general setting up a battle! Half the spice of life is not knowing what the morrow will bring—or even if you will be alive. But still, I like you better than any other woman I have known, even though you be as cold as ice to me."

"I like you, too, Nial; but not to the point of folly. Of course if you changed your ways—if you settled down, as they say— but I must not make rash promises. I pray you to escort me back to the temple."

After saying good-night to Rudabeh, Conan returned to his smithy. Finding himself bored and restless, he went down to Khesron, where in the inn he found Parvez studying a map of Zamora. To him Conan said:

"Meseems our enterprise must be done, if done it be, from the outside. The interior is too well guarded." He told of his attempt to prowl the temple corridors and his subsequent interrogation by Harpagus. "For this," he concluded, "I shall need a good length of rope—perhaps forty or fifty cubits. Do you know where I could get one?"

"Not I," said the diplomat; "but our host may. Oh, Bartakes!"

The innkeeper informed them that the nearest ropewalk was in the village of Kharshoi, a couple of leagues down the valley.

"Good," said Conan. "What would be the local price of fifty cubits thereof?" When Bartakes, after a moment of thought, named a sum, Conan held out a hand to Parvez. "Money for the rope, my lord."

"You are a hard man," said the diplomat, fumbling in his wallet. "Now you must excuse me."

With a sour glance, Parvez rose and withdrew. Left alone, Conan glanced around the common room. Captain Catigern came in, and Conan beckoned him. He and Conan ordered wine—the cheap local vintage, for Conan saw no reason to pauperize himself by buying Kyrian when he had no fair companion to savor it with. He and Catigern flipped coins for small sums.

Although Conan drank more wine than usual, Bartakes's liquor seemed to have no effect. After an hour, he and Catigern were almost where they had started, and Conan found himself more bored and restless than ever.

The taverner's daughter wandered over to watch the game. Conan yawned and said: "I've had enough, Captain. Methinks I'll to bed."

"All alone?" said Mandana archly. As Conan looked up, she met his eye and gave a little wriggle.

Conan looked at her without interest. "Smithery is hard work," he grunted. "Hammering out a sword blade is no less laborious than wielding that sword in battle. My trade has sapped my strength."

"Pooh!" retorted Mandana. "It would take more than that to tire a man of your thews! Your head is turned by that dancing girl from the temple. Think not that I did not know her when you brought her hither, for all her mummy wrappings. At least, *I* do not prance indecently around, naked but for a string of beads!"

A choking sound came from across the table, where Catigern was valiantly trying to restrain his mirth. Conan glowered at the captain, then at Bartakes' daughter, growled a curt good-night, and departed.

After Conan sought his pallet late that night, he could not sleep. All he could think of was Rudabeh; her image utterly possessed him. Although he told himself time and again that he should have nothing more to do with her—that she posed a dire threat to the freedom and independence he prized above all—still her face floated before him.

She would, he reflected, ruin him as a fighting man. She would trap him in a sticky web of domesticity, whence he could never honorably escape. Was not the spiderweb the very symbol of Yezud? He would be tied to one place and some dull trade all his life, until he was old and gray, living on soup for want of teeth to chew with. And all this when there were so many places he had not seen, and so many adventures yet untried!

But, though he recoiled with horror from the thought of spending the rest of his life as Yezud's blacksmith, an even stronger urge impelled him—a fiercely burning desire to see Rudabeh again, to gaze on her handsome face, to hear her gentle voice, to admire her proud dancer's carriage, to hold her hand. It was not mere lust, albeit he had a plenty of that.

Nor was his obsession merely a hunger for a woman—any woman. He could have enjoyed a night with the silly wench

Mandana any time he chose to pay her father's toll. But he wanted just one woman, no other.

This need, this dependence, was new to Conan's experience, and he did not altogether like it. Time and again he told himself to break out of this invisible web before it was too late. But every time he thought thus, he felt himself weakening, knowing that he could no more brusquely cast Rudabeh aside than he could bring himself to rob an old beggar.

Furthermore, he had agreed with Parvez to rescue Jamilah in return for access to the temple, where he hoped to steal the Eyes of Zath. But, if he took the Eyes, he would have to flee from Yezud as fast as a horse could carry him. If Rudabeh would flee with him—but suppose she refused? Would he give up his quest for the Eyes to settle permanently in Yezud? If he did, would either he or the girl survive Feridun's doom? It would be absurd to undertake the toil and risk of freeing Jamilah and then make no use of the Clavis of Gazrik.

His thoughts whirled round and round, like milk in a butter churn, without coming to a conclusion. At last he gave up trying to sleep and got up.

Some time after midnight, Captain Catigern inspected his Brythunian sentries. As he walked the wall of Yezud, his eye caught a distant movement on the Shadizar road. Then he sighted a man running through Khesron and up the path to the hilltop stronghold. Catigern turned sharply to the lieutenant in command of the watch, saying:

"Who's that? A messenger from the King?"

"Nay," replied the lieutenant. "Unless I mistake me, 'tis none but Nial the blacksmith. He went forth an hour since, saying he needed a good, hard run."

Conan, gasping, waited for the door in the gate valve to open. Then, still panting, he trotted through the gap, flung a surly greeting to the Brythunians, and disappeared.

"I wonder," mused the lieutenant, "has our blacksmith gone mad? Never have I seen a man run so save to escape enemies."

Catigern chuckled. "Aye, he's mad right enough—mad for a wench. Love has made men do stranger things than run a league by the light of the stars!"

IX. The Powder of Forgetfulness

During his courtship of Rudabeh, if such it could be called, Conan made preparations for sudden flight, despite the fact that he had not yet fully decided to flee. He, long accustomed to making his mind up quickly and following through his decision, right or wrong, found himself vexatiously balanced on a knife-edge of indecision.

Every day he took an hour or so off from his smithery to exercise his horse. He sharpened his sword. He mended and polished his boots, saddlery, and other equipment. He laid in a supply of durable foodstuffs: salted meat, hard biscuits, and a bag of dates brought north by traders from the Zuagir country. He borrowed Parvez's map of Zamora and studied it.

If he fled from Yezud with the Eyes of Zath, which way should he turn? To make his way back to Turan was out of the question so long as Tughril maintained his feud. He did not underestimate the sorcerous powers and lust for revenge of the High Priest of Erlik, whose son he had slain.

West of Yezud, the central ridge of the Karpash Mountains snaked north and south for many leagues. As a born hillman, Conan was sure he could cross the cliff-sided main ridge on foot, but equally sure he would have to abandon any horses he brought. He did not care to flee beyond the mountains only to find himself afoot in a strange land. Besides, if

Rudabeh decided to come with him, she also would need a mount.

He could go north to the end of the central ridge and strike west into upper Brythunia. From all he had heard, this was a poor, sparsely-settled land where, though he carried the wealth of ages, there would be nothing to spend it on. In that country he could only buy a farm and settle down to till it. To become a yeoman farmer was the least of Conan's desires; he had seen enough of peasant drudgery in his native Cimmeria.

He could push south, to the other end of the Karpashes, and strike west into Corinthia or south into Khauran. That route would take him through Shadizar, where a friendly fence would give him a handsome sum for his loot. On the other hand, too many Zamorians, from King Mithridates down, remembering his former depredations in their land, were whetting their knives for a slice of Conan's flesh. Zamora was a poor country to hide in, because Conan's very size, a head taller than most Zamorians, made him all too visible to those who sought him.

A few days after his midnight run, following a three-day absence from his smithy, Conan rode up the valley below Yezud. He was returning from the village of Kharshoi with a coil of rope tied to his saddle.

He jogged peacefully along the narrow, winding route that snaked along the side of the narrow gulch below the wider valley in which Khesron lay. The rocky sides of the valley rose steeply on either hand, carved by erosion into a confused corrugation of pinnacles and detached blocks piled helter-skelter. A fine site for an ambush, he thought, sweeping the tumbled slopes with a wary glance; the stony chaos presented an infinitude of hiding places, while no horse could negotiate such a slope without a broken leg.

Even as this thought crossed his mind, he was jerked to full alertness by a sound that his services in the Turanian army had made all too familiar: the flat snap of a bowstring, followed instantly by the whistling hiss of an arrow in flight.

Instantly, Conan threw himself forward and to the off side of the horse, since the sound came from his left, across the ravine. Holding on with one leg over the saddle and one arm around Ymir's neck, he presented but little target to the unknown archer. As he did so, the arrow sang past the place where his body had been, to shatter against the rocks on his right.

Furiously, Conan whipped back into his saddle and swept out his sword. He turned the horse, glaring at the stony slope as if by the very intensity of his blue-eyed stare he could melt the rocks that concealed his would-be assassin. His excitement communicated itself to Ymir, who danced and snorted. But nothing moved on the rocky incline before him.

He could force the horse down the short slope to the bottom of the valley and across the brook; but then he would have to dismount and climb the facing slope afoot. For a single man to charge uphill on foot, with neither shield nor armor, against a well-placed and competent archer, was equivalent to suicide. His own bow was back in its case in Yezud. For a few heartbeats he swept the rocks with his probing vision, but no sign of his attacker could he see.

At last he turned Ymir's head northward and spurred the animal toward his original destination. If he could not bring his assailant to book, he must quickly get out of range.

Hardly had the horse broken into a canter when the bow twanged again. Again, Conan ducked; but this had no effect on the arrow, which buried itself with a meaty thump in Ymir's side. The horse gave a great bound and collapsed on the edge of the roadway, rolling off and down the slope.

As his stricken steed fell, Conan flung himself clear. With catlike agility he landed on his feet; but so steep was the slope that he, too, fell and rolled. Halfway down the slope he scrambled to his feet, snatched up the scimitar he had dropped, and covered the rest of the slope in two bounds. At the bottom he jumped across the gurgling run and pounded up the other side, leaping from rock to rock. As rage was replaced by calculation, his ascent became more deliberate, taking cover behind boulders and pinnacles, scanning the slope above him, and then making a quick dash to the shelter of the next prominence.

Soon he had climbed to a level higher than that from which he had started on the other side. He could now look down upon the domes and towers of the craglets that had concealed his assailant. But no sign of his attacker could he discern, even when he had climbed to the top of the valley.

At the top, he reached a small, grassy plateau, which ran horizontally for a bowshot before rising into further slopes and peaks of the rugged Karpash foothills. He walked about the flat, frowning. Presently he sighted something that made his breath quicken: the print of a horse's hoof in a patch of sandy soil. Casting about, he found more hoof-prints and a stake driven into the ground. Evidently, some-one had recently ridden up to this plateau, bringing the stake with him. At the top he had dismounted, driven the stake into the ground, and tethered his horse while he went about his business—probably trying to put an arrow through Conan. Failing to do so, he had returned to his mount, departing in too much haste to take the stake with him.

Conan cast about, like a hound on the scent, for a clue as to his murderer's direction. But the plateau's surface was either too grassy or too stony to hold the spoor of Conan's unknown foe.

At length Conan gave up and returned down the slope to where, across the little stream, his horse lay dead. He unfas-tened the saddle and bridle and grimly set out afoot, up the slope to the road and then north toward Yezud, with rope and saddle slung over one shoulder. As he plodded, he won-dered how the assassin could have reached the top of the slope without Conan's seeing him, unless magic were involved.

This, Conan suspected, was indeed the explanation. It would not have been magic of the most fell and powerful kind, to strike Conan dead by force of a spell alone; rather it was the magic of a petty illusionist—a spell related to the hypnotic suggestions of the Vicar. For the actual killing, his attacker depended upon material weapons, using unnatural means only to keep himself hidden from Conan's sight.

Back in Yezud that evening, Conan's fury at the loss of his horse and his failure to exact payment from his attacker was mitigated by his pleasure in finding Rudabeh at her mother's house.

But Rudabeh did not look happy. "Step out into the garden, Nial," she said tensely. "I have tidings."

"Well?" asked Conan as he followed her into the cabbage patch.

"You know the Vicar, Harpagus? He has learned of our visit to Khesron."

"How so?"

"He called me in and told me that someone—he named no names, but spoke of his informant as 'she'—had carried tales to him."

"By Set!" growled Conan. "I'll wager it was that tavern slut, Mandana."

"Why should she do a thing like that? I have never harmed her."

"I think she's jealous of you, my girl; you know how women are. What does Harpagus intend?"

"He would have me yield to him that which I have denied to you. If I do not, he threatens to denounce me to Lord Feridun."

Conan's voice became the snarl of a hunting leopard. "One more score against the dog! If it wasn't he behind that attempt to murder me on the road today, I'm a Stygian!"

"What's this? Who tried to murder you?"

Briefly, Conan told the tale of his encounter on the road from Kharshoi. Rudabeh exclaimed:

"Oh, how sorry I am for the loss of your horse! But at least you survived, which is more important."

"Never mind that. What will Harpagus do if you resist?"

"It would mean death by the spider-god," said Rudabeh somberly, blanching in the ruddy light of the setting sun. "Or at least a flogging and reduction to the lowest rank in the temple service. As I see it, my choices are these: I can give in to Harpagus and, if that issues badly, end up in Zath's belly anyway. I can defy the Vicar, threatening to tell the High Priest of his lubricity. Or I can go forthwith to Feridun with my tale. But it were my word against the Vicar's, and I am sure his would prevail."

"You haven't mentioned a fourth choice: to run away with me," rumbled Conan.

She shook her head. "We have been all over that. I had almost as lief face Zath as plunge into the life you envision.

And you, too, are caught in this cleft stick; for if Feridun thought you had debauched a temple virgin, your fate would be as mine."

"Debauched!" snorted Conan. "A pretty tame sort of debauchery! Your priests, like other rulers, are wont to lay down strict rules for their subjects but themselves to do as they please."

"The rules had fallen into abeyance under Feridun's predecessor, a gluttonous voluptuary; but Feridun is a man of such stern morality that the sight of another enjoying life offends him. But about Harpagus—have you decided whither your own future lies?"

She meant: are you ready to become my prudent, unadventurous husband? Conan clenched his fists and ground his teeth with the passions that were tearing him apart. Then he had a thought that might put off the fatal decision. He said:

"Do you know of the Powder of Forgetfulness?"

"Nay. What is it?"

"A magical stuff; a witch of my acquaintance gave me some. Throw a pinch into your enemy's face, she said, and it will make him forget all about you, as if he had never heard of you. If you will step around to my chamber—" He checked himself as she began to protest. "Nay, I understand; we cannot be seen entering my place together. Wait here."

He soon returned with the pouch he had received from Nyssa. Handing it over, he sighed: "I truly love you, girl; I could show you such loving as these local clods never dreamed of."

"And what of me when you gallop off to new loves and wilder adventurers, perchance leaving me with a fatherless child?"

Conan snorted. "You, mistress, should debate with philosophers in the temple courtyards and put them all to shame! I'm no match for you in argument."

"You have a keener mind than you think; you do but lack for schooling."

"I'm schooled in handling swords and bows and horses, not in polite arts like literature."

"That can be remedied. Darius, the young priest, conducts a school for children, and he could teach you."

Conan growled: "Crom's devils, girl! Are you trying to make me over? I won't have it!"

When they tired of argument, Conan escorted Rudabeh back to the temple door. Seeing that the nighted streets were deserted, Conan seized her, crushed her to him, and covered her with burning kisses. "Come with me!" he murmured in a voice thick with passion.

When he released her, she said gently: "I confess, Nial, that I could learn to love you—but only if you would, as you say, permit me to 'make you over.' That would mean giving up your wild ways to settle in Yezud as a proper householder and husband."

Conan grunted. "I wouldn't even consider such a thing for any other woman. But for you—I'll think on it."

At his smithy the following morning, Conan gave Lar the day off and began work on a new project, which he preferred not to have the boy know about. By afternoon he had a foot-long grapnel ending in three hooks. He was securing the grapnel to his new rope by threading the rope through the eye at the other end of the grapnel and making a splice, when a tense voice called: "Nial!"

A woman stood before the open front of the smithy; Conan recognized Rudabeh despite her heavy veiling. He dropped his work and threw open the door to his private room.

"Step in," he said. "We cannot talk here where everybody can see us. Fear not for your cursed virtue." When both were in the room, he closed the door. "Now what's happened?"

"There is such confusion at the temple that I knew none would miss me."

"Yes, yes; but what's up?"

"Your powder worked—if anything, too well. Harpagus came to my cubicle today, bolted the door, and began his advances by threats and wheedling intermixed. When he laid lustful hands upon me, I raised the pouch and threw the contents in his face."

"A pinch would have sufficed."

The girl shrugged. "Doubtless; but in the excitement I could not measure out the dose with such nicety. He sneezed and coughed and wiped his eyes; and when he had finished

he gazed upon me blankly, with no more guile in his face
than a babe's! Then he asked me who and where he was.
Here's your empty pouch."

"Crom, the powder seems to have blasted his mind for
fair! What then?"

"I pushed him out of the room, and he wandered off muttering. I heard that other priests found him thus and took
him to the High Priest, who tried by his arcane arts to restore
the Vicar's memory. But at last accounts he had not succeeded. I am truly grateful, dear Nial—"

Conan interrupted: "Then there's a favor you can do me in
return—oh, not what you're thinking," he added as she
shrank away, "although I hope we shall come to that, too.
Right now I must know where the Turanian woman is kept
captive."

"I must not reveal the temple's secrets—" began Rudabeh.

"Nonsense!" growled Conan. "Haven't you learned that
priests are as avid for their own selfish pleasure as other
men? The lady is but a pawn in Feridun's play for unlimited
power, and I must learn where she abides. Besides, I'm not a
stranger; I work for the temple just as you do. Now will you
tell me, girl?"

"Well—ah—know you the second story at the north end
of the temple?"

"Aye; from a distance I have seen windows high up all the
way round the temple."

"The lady is in a chamber on that level, betwixt the north-
ernmost of the west wings and the wing next to it."

"Like this?" Conan squatted on the floor and drew lines in
the dust with his finger.

"Exactly! The wall runs from one wing to the other,
enclosing a three-sided space below the chamber."

"What's behind that wall? A pleasure garden?"

"Nay; there Feridun keeps his pet Hyrkanian tiger, called
Kirmizi. Therefore, when the priests wish to isolate a guest,
they house him in that apartment."

Conan grunted. "A tiger, eh? A nice tame kitty?"

"Nay; he's a fierce creature, who can be governed only by
the High Priest. Lord Feridun has magical powers over animals. It may be merely a coincidence, but when he and the
priest Zariadris were competing for the post of High Priest,

and Feridun was elected, Zariadris set out for Shadizar to protest to the King that the election had been fraudulent. He was dragged from his horse by wolves and devoured. Surely you do not plan—"

"Never mind what I plan," grunted Conan. "You'd better start for your mother's house; I'll join you there."

Late that night, the pale face of the full moon gazed down upon Conan of Cimmeria as he cautiously moved around the great wall of the temple. When he came to the section enclosing the area beneath Jamilah's chamber, he uncoiled the rope he carried and tossed the grapnel over the top of the wall. On his second try, the hooks caught.

It was but the work of a moment for the Cimmerian to clamber up the rope and balance himself on the top of the wall. He glanced down into the thoroughfare; but the streets of Yezud were deserted. With no alehouses or other places of public entertainment, most of the citizens retired early. The town watch had already made its nightly sweep of the streets, and had disbanded and gone home, while Catigern's Brythunians on night duty were posted around the city wall or else inside the temple. Yezud had so little crime that no massive precautions against it were deemed necessary.

Conan then studied the triangular area bounded by the wall and the adjacent wings of the temple. Trees and shrubs cast velvety shadows, black pools in the moonlight. Conan's keen vision roved the ground until it lighted upon a bulk lying stretched out beneath a tree.

As if sensing Conan's gaze upon it, the beast heaved itself to its feet and took a step toward the wall, which Conan straddled. From the tiger's throat issued a prolonged grunt—a sound like that of a saw cutting through a log.

An upward glance told Conan that the window of Jamilah's room was thrice man-height above the ground of Kirmizi's enclosure. As the tiger advanced, Conan wrenched his grapnel out of the masonry and leaped to the ground outside the wall. Coiling his rope again, he headed back toward the smithy.

X. The Tiger's Fang

The following noon, Conan strode into Bartakes's Inn.
Seated at a small table, Parvez was bent over a board game
with Psamitek, the Stygian scholar. Save for two of Parvez's
Turanian retainers and a trader from the South, the common
room was otherwise deserted. As Conan approached, the
diplomat and the scholar looked up.

"Greeting, friend Nial!" said Parvez. "You have been
exercising your steed?"

"I would have been; but, two days since, some swine shot
the poor beast dead under me. That's not what I came to tell
you, though." He looked significantly at Psamitek.

"You must excuse us," said Parvez to the Stygian. "Let
Chagor take my side of the game."

Psamitek rose, bowed, murmured an apology, and carried
the game board away, holding it carefully level so that the
pieces should not slide off. Presently he and Chagor had
their heads close together over the board, scowling at the
pieces and occasionally making a move.

Conan sat down on the vacant stool and in a low voice
said: "I have found out about your captive princess." He told
the Turanian of his cursory investigation of the night before.

"A tiger, eh?" mused the Turanian. "To one of your thews,
slaying such a beast were not impossible."

"No, thank you!" growled Conan. "I once slew a lion under similar circumstance, in the grounds of a sorcerer who used such cats as watchdogs: But my success was more one of luck than of skill. I came closer to entering the land of the shades at that moment than in any of my brawls and battles."

"What, then, do you propose?" asked Parvez. "To seek the lady's chamber through the interior of the temple?"

"Not with the corridors crawling with guards, as they are day and night. Have you some magical means to slay this tiger, or at least cast it into a deep slumber?"

"Alas, no! I do not traffic in magic, save for that silver arrow you extorted from me. Now that I think, I do have a means for immobilizing Feridun's striped pet." He fumbled in his scrip and brought out a phial containing a greenish liquid. "An accessory of my trade; three drops of this in a man's drink will waft him to dreamland for hours. But I know not how we shall persuade the tiger to consume the stuff—"

"That's easy," said Conan. "Wait here."

He pushed through the door of the kitchen, where he found Bartakes laboring over provisions for the evening's cookery. When the innkeeper looked up, Conan asked: "Mine host, have you a stout roast of beef, uncooked, that you will sell?"

"What—ah—what in the nine hells do you want with—" began Bartakes, but under Conan's baleful glare he changed his tune. "Well, yes I have. It will cost—"

"The lord Parvez will pay," said Conan, jerking his thumb toward the door to the common room. "Fetch it; he and I are planning a surprise party for a friend."

Bartakes disappeared and shortly returned bearing a platter, on which reposed a haunch of beef large enough to feed a score of warriors. He set it on a vacant table and went out to collect the price from Parvez.

Drawing his scimitar, Conan made a series of cuts into the beef, as deep as the width of his blade. Then he sprinkled the contents of the phial into the cuts. While he was doing this, Bartakes returned.

"What is that?" asked the taverner. "Some kind of seasoning?"

"Aye; a rare condiment from a far land. Now, have you some sacking in which to wrap this thing?"

When the beef had been packaged; Conan returned to the common room with the bundle on his shoulder, pausing at Parvez's table. The diplomat whispered: "When do you plan your attempt?"

"Tonight. We have no time to dawdle; the priests are suspicious of me already. Have you something I can show the lady, to prove I am not merely one more abductor?"

"Take this," said Parvez, pulling off a seal ring and handing it to Conan. "It will identify you."

Conan slipped the ring over his little finger and, carrying the raw beef swathed in sacking over his shoulder, marched out.

The moon, barely past full, thrust its silvern beams through rents in the cloud-crowded sky. It had not yet reached the meridian when Conan, moving quietly down the deserted street, reached the wall that bounded Kirmizi's domain. Halting, he grasped the raw meat with both hands and, whirling it twice about, with a mighty heave sent it soaring across the barrier. It landed inside with a moist thump. Instantly came the grunt of an aroused tiger, and then rending and slobbering sounds told of the beast's enjoyment of the unexpected meal.

Conan squatted in the angle of the wall that furnished the deepest shadow against the light of the fickle moon. With the patience of a hunter in the wild, there he remained, immobile and scarcely breathing, while the moon pursued her cloud-enshrouded path toward the western horizon.

When Conan's ears at last picked up the wheezy sounds of a colossal yawn, he took off his boots and hitched his baldric around so that his sword hung down between his massive shoulders. Pausing no longer, he uncoiled his rope, flung the grapnel over the wall, and swarmed up to the top.

For a moment he could make out nothing in the night-drenched darkness below, for a large, dense cloud had cast the temple and its environs into shadow. When the moon peeped through again, she showed the tiger stretched out peacefully, head on paws and eyes closed. Glancing up at the broken sky, Conan was unpleasantly reminded of the night he had scaled the wall to Narkia's apartment. He wondered if there were some omen in this celestial aspect.

At last he whistled softly, then waited. When the beast still did not stir, Conan loosened his grapnel, lowered himself down the inner side of the wall until he hung by his huge hands, then dropped the remaining distance. Kirmizi slumbered on.

Warily, Conan surveyed the occupant of the pen. The tiger lay motionless save for the slow rise and fall of its ribs. While Conan could clearly discern its black stripes, the orange-red of its fur was faded to tarnished silver by the uncertain moonlight.

Beyond the sleeping cat rose the narrow expanse of masonry that separated the inner ends of the two adjacent wings of the temple. An iron gate, set in this wall at ground level, permitted entry and egress for him who tended to the tiger's needs; while, directly above this gate, the window of Jamilah's chamber, the shutters of which were open to the warm summer breezes, formed a black rectangular patch in the dimly reflective marble of the temple wall. No lights were to be seen.

A gliding shadow, Conan stole past the sleeping tiger to the apex of the enclosure. Again he uncoiled his rope and, whirling the trefoil grapnel round and round, sent it flying toward the dark aperture above. At the first throw, the grapnel struck the wall with a metallic clank, loud in the stillness, and fell back to earth. A second throw accomplished no more.

As he coiled the rope for another try, Conan cursed himself for not having practiced this maneuver before attempting it in earnest. A third throw sent the grapnel into the window, but the hooks failed to catch when Conan pulled on the free end. His fourth attempt succeeded.

Conan hoisted himself up, hand over hand, while the bulging muscles of his arms writhed like pythons. He clambered over the sill and landed on the uncarpeted floor with a faint slap of bare feet.

The vagrant moon shot a narrow beam of silver slantwise through the window, where it cast an oblong of argent upon the silken hangings of the chamber. The faint illumination outlined a bedstead on which lay a slender form. The night

being warm, the sleeper had thrown back the coverlet, dis-
closing to the Cimmerian's probing gaze the graceful body
of a woman, whose dark hair fell loosely across her opalescent shoulders and parted to reveal the pale moons of her
splendid breasts.

Conan glided to the bed and whispered: "Lady Jamilah!"

The woman slept on. Conan grasped the curve of her soft
shoulder and gently shook her, whereupon Jamilah's eyes
slowly opened. Then her eyelids fluttered, and her lips
parted with a sharp intake of breath. Conan clapped a broad
hand over her mouth to smother her scream; all that emerged
was a faint gurgle.

"Hush, lady!" he hissed. "I'm here to rescue you!"

He raised his hand from the pale oval of her face, holding
it close enough to clap it down again.

"Who—who are you?" she whispered at last.

"Call me Nial," growled Conan. "King Yildiz's ambassador, Lord Parvez, has sent me to get you out of here. He
waits nearby."

"How know I that you speak true?"

Conan pulled off the seal ring and thrust it at her. "He
gave me this to show you. It's too dark to see the design on
the seal, but you can feel it with your thumb."

She fondled the ring. "How did you enter here?"

"Through the window."

"But the tiger?"

"Kirmizi sleeps with a drug in his belly. Come! You'll
have to trust me, unless you'd liefer remain a prisoner here."

Suddenly conscious of her nudity, Jamilah reached for the
coverlet. "I cannot rise, with you staring down at me! Turn
your back at least."

"Women!" grunted Conan disgustedly. "With our lives
hanging on one thread, this is no time for your civilized
niceties." But he went to the window and stared out, listen-
ing alertly lest Jamilah, moved by doubts about the truth of
his tale, attempt to stab him in the back. There he heard
nothing but the rustle of rich attire hastily donned. At last
Jamilah murmured:

"You may turn, Master Nial. What would you now?"

Conan hauled in his rope; and when it was neatly coiled
upon the chamber floor, he tied a loop in the free end and
lowered this oval an arm's length down the wall outside.

"Wait," he said. "Have you a proper cloak, besides those frilly garments? If you're seen in the street . . . ."

"I understand." She went to a chest and brought out a black velvet cloak with a hood. She handed the bundle to Conan, who tossed it out the window, taking care that it should not strike the sleeping tiger.

"Come here," he said. "Sit on the casement sill, and I'll support you while you place your feet in the loop. Do not look down, but hold my arm while you feel for the rope. There! Now grasp the rope with both hands."

"The rough rope pricks my fingers," complained Jamilah as she lowered herself into position. "And heights do terrify me."

"That cannot be helped, lady. Steady, now; here we go!"

Hand over hand, Conan paid out the rope until the princess reached the ground. Then he examined the hook of the grapnel, which was firmly embedded in the wood of the windowsill. If he lowered himself by the way he had come up, Conan realized that he would be unable to dislodge the rope by jerking it from below, and he needed the rope to get himself and Jamilah over the outer wall of the enclosure.

At last he pulled the entire rope back into the chamber, wrenched the hook out of the sill, and dragged the massive bed across the floor to the window. He passed one end of the rope around the nearest bedpost and hauled briskly until the bight of the rope was at the center of its length.

Dropping the two free ends over the windowsill and firmly gripping the two strands together, he lowered himself over the sill and rappelled down until he hung just above the ground. Then he released the looped end and dropped, as lithely as a pouncing panther, to the ground, and pulled on the grapnel end of the rope until the entire rope tumbled down upon him.

He found a terrified Jamilah pressed back against the wall, gazing wide-eyed at the tiger, whose heavy odor filled his nostrils. Hastily coiling the rope and picking up the woman's cloak, Conan threw a protective arm around the fear-frozen woman and, shadow-silent on the greensward, walked her past the slumbering Kirmizi.

At the outer wall, Conan whirled his grapnel once again and again caught it in the masonry. As he prepared to ascend, a sudden intake of Jamilah's breath warned him of impending danger. Whirling, he saw the tiger rise on unsteady paws and stalk toward him. Evidently the soporific dose had not been adequate, even though he had emptied Parvez's flask into the cloven meat.

Conan swept out his scimitar as the beast, with a rumbling snarl, broke into a lope and, like a coiled spring released, leaped straight at him, its great jaws open and slavering. As the giant cat, fangs bared and talons unsheathed, hurtled toward him, Conan whipped his scimitar up over his head and, with legs braced and both powerful hands gripping the hilt, brought the heavy curved blade whistling down between the glowing emerald eyes. The tiger's body slammed into him and hurled him back against the wall, so that man and tiger fell in a tangled heap at the foot of the enclosure.

As Conan's body disappeared beneath the striped form, Jamilah stifled a little shriek, clapping a jeweled hand over her mouth. "Are you dead, Nial?" she breathed.

"Not quite," grumbled Conan, crawling out from under the limp carcass like an insect emerging from under a stone. Rising, he looked down upon the animal, which lay prone with Conan's scimitar still fixed in its cloven skull. With one bare foot planted on the tiger's head, Conan tugged with all his might to wrench the weapon free.

"Damn!" he muttered. "I swore that never again would I be caught in such a fix; so much for mortal plans. At least this good Kothian steel survived the blow."

"Are you hurt?" inquired Jamilah, her low-pitched voice vibrant with concern.

"I think no bones are broken, albeit I have scratches and bruises aplenty. I feel like a man who has run the gauntlet between lines of foes with clubs."

He wiped his sword on the tiger's fur and sheathed it. Then, climbing the rope to the top of the wall, he sat astride it to haul the princess up and lower her down the other side. At last he released the rope from its attachment in the masonry and dropped down himself. He pulled on his boots, saying:

"Put on the cloak, and pull the hood well down. There will be guards at the city gate, so you'll have to play the part of my sweetheart—one of the village girls from Khesron. Do you understand?"

"I trust, Master Nial," she said, "that you do not plan some improper liberty. After all, I am of royal rank."

"Fear not; but you'll have to forget your royal rank if you want to get away from Yezud!"

"But—"

"But me no buts, lady! Your choice is between staying here and doing what I tell you. Make up your mind."

"Oh, very well," she said. Limping from his bruises, Conan hustled the noblewoman away.

As they passed another of the walls connecting the end of adjacent wings of the temple, Conan suddenly halted, also stopping Jamilah.

"What is it?" she whispered.

"Listen!" He put his ear against the stone, motioning her to silence.

From the enclosure on the other side of this wall came two voices in grave discussion. Conan picked out the deep, bell-like tones of High Priest Feridun; the other voice he could not identify but assumed to be that of a lesser priest. The High Priest said:

". . . fear me the Children will not have reached their full growth for several months."

"But, Holiness!" said the other voice. "We cannot continue to put off the King with bootless threats. He thinks we do but try to frighten him with imaginary bogles."

"But my dear Mirzes, it is not we but he who is bluffing. Well he knows that let his raggle-taggle army but sight one of the Children of Zath, they will dissolve in panic flight. We have the most terrible weapon since the invention of the sword."

"How shall we convince him?"

"Another embassy will soon arrive. If all else fails, I shall take Mithridates's envoy below and show him."

"Suppose he still rejects our just demands?"

"Then we shall set the Great Plan in motion. Even if not fully grown, the Children will perform their duty."

"Zath grant that all work as planned, master," murmured the priest Mirzes.

"Fear not," replied Feridun's tolling voice. "I can govern the Children, as I can beasts of all kinds. As my new Vicar, you must trust me to know best . . . ."

The voices faded away, as if the speakers were withdrawing into the temple. Conan motioned to Jamilah to resume their progress. But the delicate, highborn Turanian woman found it hard to keep up with Conan's lengthy stride, and her thin slippers slipped on the rounded cobblestones.

"Here, let me carry you!" muttered Conan. When she uttered some faint protest, he swept her off her feet and pounded toward the city gate.

Soon afterward, as the moon hung low over the Karpashes, Conan astonished the Brythunians at the front gate by appearing, carrying the cloak-wrapped form of a woman. He set her on her feet but kept one brawny arm around her waist. He whispered in her ear:

"Now play your part, damn it; but don't speak! They'd catch your accent."

"Nial the lady-killer, at it again!" smirked one of the guards.

"Keep it quiet, lads," said Conan. "I'm taking her home; but her people are narrow-minded."

He tightened his grip on Jamilah's waist with a little jerk. She forced a giggle and leaned her head on Conan's shoulder. At a ribald remark from the other guard about what she and Conan had been doing, he felt her stiffen with indignation. But then they were through the small door and moving swiftly down the long incline to the bottom of the crag.

A thunderous knocking on the front door of his inn aroused Bartakes. He dragged himself out of bed to shout imprecations down from his bedroom window, adding: "Any fool can see we are closed for the night!"

Conan roared back: "I don't want you; I want Lord Parvez. Rouse him, unless you wish me to tear down your pigsty board by board! Tell him there's a noble traveler here."

Moments later, the yawning Turanian appeared at the door, clutching his flowered night robe about him.

"Here she is," said Conan's rough voice, "sound but weary."

Parvez dropped to one knee. "My lady Jamilah!" he exclaimed. "Come in at once!" A tear glistened on his cheek in the moonlight, so strong was his emotion. Rising, he said to Conan: "You have done the miraculous, young man. May I have my seal ring back, pray?"

"Oh, I forgot about it," said Conan slipping off the ring and handing it over.

"And one more thing. Have you seen my servant Chagor?"

"No, I have not. What of him?"

"The fellow has vanished, with his horse. No explanation. Ah, well; I must now bid you a hasty farewell, for it would not do to be here when the priests discover their captive has been enlarged. Bartakes, be so good as to rouse my retainers; we must be on the road ere dawn."

"Permit me to thank you, Master Nial," said Jamilah. "If ever you come to Turan, feel free to ask a boon of me, and if possible I will persuade the King to grant it. Farewell!" She disappeared into the inn.

Back at his quarters, Conan caught a little sleep and was lustily banging away at his anvil next morning when a party of four priests and two Brythunian soldiers appeared before his smithy. A priest in a scarlet turban and a dark-blue robe stepped into the smithy and, raising his voice above the clang of the hammer, said in a sharp, abrupt manner:

"You are Nial the blacksmith, are you not? A lady has been abducted. Hast seen such a person?"

"What sort of lady?" growled Conan, keeping his eyes on his workpiece. After a few more blows he returned it to the furnace and turned to face his questioner.

"Tall, black-haired, and fair to see," said the priest, "albeit past her thirtieth year."

Conan shook his head. "I know naught of such a woman."

"Moreover, Ambassador Parvez and his Turanians hastily departed from Khesron last night. What know you of that?"

"Again, naught. I knew the man; we sometimes drank together of an evening."

"What did you and he talk about?"

"Horses and swords and such things."

"Someone," persisted the priest in a hectoring tone, "slew the High Priest's tiger with a single mighty blow of a sword or axe. Who but you has the thews for such a blow?"

Conan shrugged. "Many Brythunians are large, strong men. To you Zamorians, anyone else looks like a mountain of muscle. As for me, this is the first I have heard of it."

"All barbarians are liars!" sneered the priest. "Fear not, we will get to the bottom of this, and you had better be ready to prove your innocence." He took a step forward and thrust his face close to Conan's.

Conan picked his workpiece out of the furnace with tongs and held the ruddily glowing iron before him. "Be careful around a forge, friend priest. If you get too close, this may set your whiskers afire." When the priest hastily backed away, Conan laid the piece on the anvil and resumed his pounding.

The priest turned and rejoined his group, who marched away. Lar, who had watched the exchange big-eyed, said: "Oh, Master Nial, you all but defied the priests of Zath! They can call upon divine powers to blast you, if you use them with insolence!"

"What's the name of the one who questioned me just now?" growled Conan.

"That is the holy father Mirzes."

"I thought I knew the voice," mused Conan. "He's the new Vicar, I hear. Come on, lad; put some thews into working the bellows! Your fire is barely hot enough to boil water."

XI. The Stench of Carrion

For several days Conan did not see Rudabeh, save when she danced during a service to Zath. He entered the temple early, so as to stand in the front row, whence he had the best view of the spider-idol. Since this was a fair day and sunlight came through the clerestory windows above, Conan could clearly make out the four Eyes across the front of the creature, even at a distance of twenty cubits.

The barbarian's keen vision caught sight of a thin ring around each Eye, lighter in color than the black stone of the statue. This, Conan reasoned, must be a ring of metal or cement let into the stone to hold the gem in place. To remove the Eyes he would have to dislodge these retaining rings, and do so very gently, so as not to crack the jewels. Conan had a good working knowledge of gems from his days as a thief, and he knew the fragility of opals.

Meanwhile his passion for Rudabeh, instead of subsiding, tormented him more and more. When Amytis told him that she expected her daughter home for supper, he impatiently awaited her in the garden, brooding.

On one hand, a fierce desire, like a tornado whirling along its serpentine path of destruction, surged up within him, to give up his rootless, adventurous life, to wed Rudabeh according to the laws of Zamora, and to become, as best he might, a solid citizen who cherished his growing family,

116

joined the municipal watch, worshiped at the temple, and paid his tithes.

Yet, on the other hand, Conan's wild, free, undisciplined spirit recoiled from this tableau as from a venomous serpent. But his other choice was to forget the girl and flee instanter, with the Eyes of Zath if he could obtain them, without them if he could not. If Feridun loosed his promised devastation upon the land, he might have to flee anyway, with or without Rudabeh.

When she appeared, he held out his arms. She shook her head, saying: "Do not torment me, Nial. I do truly love you, but you know under what conditions I would give myself to you."

"But, my girl—" began Conan. She held up a hand saying: "I have news of moment. You've heard of the disappearance of the princess Jamilah?"

"Aye; some such gossip has smitten my ears."

"The High Priest is furious, as you might expect. Some of the priests suspect you of complicity."

"Who, me?" said Conan, with an air of injured innocence. "What have I to do with a Turanian noble-woman?"

"They know you were thick with that diplomat at Bartakes's Inn, who vanished the same night as Jamilah. You would have been seized already, but that Feridun insists he have solid evidence against you ere he acts. I must say the old man tries to live up to his principles."

"Furthermore," continued Rudabeh, "if gossip be true, the High Priest has advanced the date of his revolution. He held Jamilah as a hostage for the good conduct of the king of Turan. Now he must needs move quickly ere the Turanians learn of the princess's escape. So he has warned all the temple folk to hold themselves ready seven days hence. When the alarm gong sounds, we must all go to our quarters and bolt ourselves in."

Conan grunted as he digested this information. He must, he thought, get rid of that telltale coil of rope before some snooping priest stumbled upon it.

Amytis called, and they went in for supper. Afterwards, Conan escorted Rudabeh back to the temple and took his way to Khesron. He would have to plan his raid on the temple quickly, and he thought he could map his campaign best sitting alone with a stoup of wine before him.

"Hail, Nial!" At the inn, Catigern's booming voice jogged Conan's elbow. "How about a game?" The Brythunian rattled a pair of dice in his fist.

"I thank you, but not tonight," said Conan. "I need to be alone."

Catigern shrugged and went off to seek other companionship. Conan resumed his broodings. Several jacks of wine later, another voice, with a slight lisp and a guttural accent, invaded his musings. It was Psamitek the Stygian.

"Master Nial," said the slim, swarthy scholar. "Someone wishes to see you beyond the inn."

"Well," growled Conan ungraciously, "tell that someone to come in. He can see me better here in the light."

The scholar smiled a crooked little smile. "It is a lady," he murmured. "It would not be proper for her to enter a vulgar barrel house like this."

"Lady?" grunted Conan. "What the devil . . . ." He rose, wondering if Jamilah, for some unaccountable reason, had returned to Khesron; but no, that would be insane. He followed Psamitek out.

In the courtyard of Bartakes's Inn, illuminated by the bitumen lamp over the front door and the light of the gibbous moon, stood Rudabeh. Conan gasped as he viewed her; for, instead of the modest street garb she normally wore outside the temple, she was clad in her dancing costume of a few strings of beads and nothing else.

"Conan, darling!" she said in a low, thrilling voice. "You were right and I was wrong. Come, and I will show you that I am as much a woman as you are a man. I know a place where the grass is thick and soft."

She turned and walked deliberately out of the courtyard, while Conan followed like a man in a daze. In the back of his mind, reason tried to warn him that all was not as it seemed; but the warning was swept aside by his rising tide of passion. His blood roared in his ears.

Rudabeh led Conan past a few hovels and out of the village. Her well-rounded form swayed seductively as she walked. Away from the houses of Khesron, the stony ground sloped up, and Conan became impatient to reach the promised meadow.

The ground leveled again, and Rudabeh turned to face Conan. She held out welcoming arms—and in that instant she disappeared. In her place stood Chagor the Turanian, Parvez's vanished retainer, whom Conan had bathed in the horse trough. Chagor held a thick, double-curved Hyrkanian compound bow, with an arrow drawn to the head.

"Ha!" cried the Turanian. "Now you see!" And he released his shaft with the same sharp, flat twang that Conan had heard when he lost his horse. At that range it was impossible to miss.

But as Chagor let fly his shaft, something flew from behind Conan and struck the Turanian with a thump in the chest. As a result, the arrow whistled past Conan's ear.

Before Chagor could whip another shaft from his quiver, Conan swept out his scimitar and charged with the roar of an angry lion. The Turanian dropped his bow and likewise drew, just in time to meet Conan's rush.

Steel clanged and scraped in the moonlight. Behind him, Conan heard sounds of struggle but had no leisure to investigate. The Turanian was a strong swordsman, and Conan found his hands full. Slash backhand—parry—a forehand cut—parry—feint—parry. . . . The dancing blades clashed, ground, and twirled to the accompaniment of the stamp of booted feet, heavy breathing, and muttered curses.

The curses were Chagor's, for Conan fought in grim silence. Chagor gasped. "I show you, dog. . . . Your head go to priest of Erlik. . . . Then me rich, you dead. . . ."

Once Chagor was a fraction slow in bringing his blade to a proper parry. Conan's heavier sword sliced into his forearm. Uttering a yell of dismay, Chagor dropped his scimitar. With a catlike leap, Conan sprang forward and, with the power born of frenzy, swung his sword in a wide horizontal arc. The blade sheared through the Turanian's thick neck; his head flew off, to land like a thrown melon in a nearby clump of shrubbery. The body, spouting a fountain of blood, black in the moonlight, tumbled to earth like a felled tree.

At the continuing sounds of struggle behind him, Conan whirled and perceived a tangle of limbs, which resolved itself into Captain Catigern struggling on the ground with Psamitek the Stygian.

Conan seized one of the Stygian's arms with his free hand and twisted. Between him and Catigern, they subdued the scholar, who sat up with his arms gripped behind him and Catigern's dagger pricking his throat.

"How came you to help me so timely?" asked Conan.

"I saw you follow this dog out," explained Catigern, "after you said you wished to be alone; so I became suspicious. I never trusted this Stygian dung; and the next thing I saw was you following Chagor up the hill, bleating endearments, while Psamitek followed you, mumbling some spell. Since this did not sound like you, Nial, I followed Psamitek. When the Turanian drew an arrow on you, I cast a stone to spoil his aim and went for the Stygian. Have a care with this devil; he's stronger than he looks. He bit me."

"All right, Psamitek," said Conan. "Explain this business. There's a small chance that, if we like your explanation, we'll let you live."

"You heard Chagor," said Psamitek. "He overheard Ambassador Parvez address you as 'Conan,' and I knew about Tughril's offer for Conan's head. So we put *our* heads together and arranged that he should desert Parvez's escort, and we should divide the reward betwixt us. Even your limited minds could grasp this simple scheme. . . ."

Psamitek's hypnotic voice so absorbed the attention of Conan and Catigern that they relaxed their grip upon him. Instantly the Stygian, lithe as an eel, squirmed out of their grasp and sprang to his feet. Conan leaped up, swinging his scimitar in a blow that would have cut the slender Stygian in two.

But the blade only swished through empty air. Psamitek had vanished like a blown-out candle flame.

"Come back here!" roared Conan, rushing this way and that with his blade bared and crashing through thorny bushes. The only reply was a peal of cynical, mocking laughter.

"You have your tricks, Conan," said the lisping voice, "but I have mine also, as you shall yet see. Farewell, barbarian lout!"

Conan dashed toward the voice, his sword cleaving the air; but he found nothing. Catigern said: "Save your breath, Nial. The fellow is evidently an expert caster of illusions, and he has made himself invisible. What's this about your being Conan, with a price on your head?"

"You should know better than to ask a fellow-mercenary about his past," growled Conan.

"True; forget what I said. We had better drag the Turanian's remains back to the village. The priests will want another report."

"Why not leave him for the hyenas?"

"His ghost would haunt us."

"Oh, very well," said Conan, grasping one ankle of the corpse and dragging it. "You can carry the head, though I'd rather send it as a gift to Tughril. And thanks for saving my life."

As the Festival of All Gods approached, the temple of Zath hummed with activity. Rudabeh's time was taken up with her duties, so Conan had no more personal meetings with her. Bartakes's Inn filled up with the retinues of priestly parties from far parts of Zamora, and latecomers were obliged to rent space in the cramped houses of the villagers or pitch tents in the surrounding fields.

The festival began three days after the slaying of Chagor. Delegations from opulent sanctuaries and lowly shrines of the various Zamorian gods paraded up the broad steps of the temple with pomp and ceremony. Catigern's Brythunians, their polished mail flashing in the sun, stood facing one another in two lines at opposite ends of the temple steps. As each pontiff, in glittering robe and jewel-bedight headdress, marched slowly up the stairs, the soldiers raised their pikes and halberds in salute, then grounded their weapons with a thunderous crash. The priesthoods of the different deities were riven by venomous rivalries, Conan knew, and ceaselessly intrigued to damage one another. But for today each legate beamed upon his fellow clerics and bowed benignly to the assembled priests of Zath.

During the procession of the priests, Conan stood in an inconspicuous corner of the square that fronted on the temple. But after the entrance of the last delegation, when the folk of Yezud and the spellbound pilgrims streamed in to honor the assembled gods of the Zamorian pantheon, Conan mingled with the motley crowd. In the vestibule he thought of slipping away for another attempt to explore the corridors; but this was impossible with a Brythunian firmly planted in front of the entrance to each hallway. So Conan resigned himself to standing through one more endless suite of rituals.

He took a place at the rear of the naos and stood through three hours of ceremony, in which the high priests of the other gods took turns invoking their deities and begging them for favors. Conan ignored their pronouncements but admired the glitter of their bejewelled regalia. If he could only strip a few of these pontiffs of their robes and miters, he thought, the jewels in them would ease his life for years, even though their value would be but a fraction of that of the Eyes of Zath.

Two days later, shafts of rain, hurled from a leaden sky, flogged the worn cobblestones of Yezud as the Festival of All Gods ended. The visiting priests, wrapped in voluminious hooded cloaks against the rain, bid ceremonious farewells to Feridun and his new Vicar on the steps of the temple before turning away to take their places in carriages and horse litters or to mount horses, mules, and camels.

That night, while rain still fell, a giant figure in a dark cloak slipped through the streets of Yezud on noiseless moccasins. At the southernmost wing on the east side of the temple of Zath, Conan fumbled for the silver arrow he had received from Parvez. Touching the lock with the point, he murmured: *"Kapinin achilir genishi!"*

A faint, rusty squeal, as if someone within were turning a key in the long-disused lock, made itself heard above the patter of rain. Conan pushed the door, but it failed to open.

Angrily, Conan threw his great weight against the door, striking it with his massive shoulder. Still it did not yield. Then he paused to think.

Perhaps the priests, not trusting in an ordinary lock alone, also warded the door with an inside bolt, like that outside the portal on the other side of the temple, into which the sheep had been driven. Pointing the silver arrow at various heights, Conan repeated *kapinin achilir genishi* several times. At last he was rewarded by the muffled clank of a bolt's being thrown back. At his next push, the door opened.

The hall inside was dark, save for a rectangle of dim light thirty cubits away, where this passage joined the main circumferential corridor. Conan paused to listen; the temple was as silent as a Stygian tomb. The temple people from High Priest to slaves must be sleeping a sleep of exhaustion after the last three days' activities.

Conan stole down the hall, alert for a sign of the Brythunian guards. Cautiously he peeked around corners at the end, but no guards did he see in the main corridor in either direction. As he had hoped, the guards were taking advantage of their employers' fatigue to cluster somewhere, perhaps in the vestibule, for gaming and talk, rather than spend the night in lonely patrolling of the silent hallways.

The corridor into which Conan emerged was lit by a single bitumen lamp in a wall bracket. He turned right and, continuing his strides, walked to a door on the left. If his estimates of distance had been correct, this should be one of the side entrances to the naos.

Again he applied the Clavis of Gazrik to the door and whispered the incantation; again the lock unlocked itself, with no sound except a well-oiled click. When he opened the door, though, he recoiled. Instead of the naos, he found himself surveying a small bedchamber occupied by two narrow bunks, on which lay a pair of acolytes, one snoring. Conan softly closed the door and stole away.

The next door proved to be the one he sought. He slipped into the naos and hurried across the floor of the sanctum, fitfully illuminated by the flickering orange light of the eternal flame. He stopped at the black stone statue of Zath.

Again he was struck by the lifelike aspect of the carving. The work was a perfect replica of a giant arachnid, save that the sculptor, unable to reproduce in stone the hairs along the legs, had indicated them by cross-hatching.

Conan stripped off his cloak and dropped it. Beneath it he wore his blacksmith's apron, with pockets and loops holding the tools of his trade. He pulled out his blacksmith's hammer and, holding his breath for instant flight, gingerly tapped the nearest leg. The sound was reassuringly like that of honest stone; the statue showed no sign of animation.

Conan moved closer to reach the front of the creature's body. The four forward Eyes gleamed in the wavering light of the eternal flame, so that a six-rayed crimson star seemed to dance in the blue-green mistiness of each Eye.

Conan saw that he would need a stronger light than that of the burning bitumen to operate on the Eyes. Reaching under his apron, he brought out a stick of wood, a cubit in length, one end of which was wrapped in an oil-soaked rag. Moving to the luminous bowl that sheltered the eternal fire, he held the unguent-coated cloth on the end of his torch above the lambent flame until the oil caught fire and blazed up.

Conan returned to the statue and wedged his torch into the angle between two of Zath's eight legs, so that it cast a wavering yellow light upon the Eyes on that side. He leaned forward to examine the Eyes, running his fingers over their smooth, spherical surfaces and feeling the retaining rings that held them in place. The Eyes were girasols as large as a small boy's fist. The retaining rings were of lead. This, thought Conan, should make his task easy.

From a pocket of his apron he brought out a handful of drills and stylets. Among these he chose a flat drill with a narrow chisel point. Setting the point into the crack between one of the retaining rings and the surrounding stone, he gave a gentle tap with his hammer, then another. He rejoiced to see that the tool had sunk visibly into the lead; a few more taps and he should be able to pry the ring out.

Sounds from without snatched Conan's attention away from the statue. Voices murmured, feet tramped, doors opened and shut. Amid the sounds, Conan thought he detected the clank of the Brythunians' arms. Now what in the nine hells was arousing the temple at this hour?

Then a key clicked in the side door facing that through which he had come. Before he could retreat, the door swung open.

Snatching his tools away from the statue, Conan whirled, lips drawn back in a voiceless snarl. When he saw Rudabeh in the doorway, he growled: "What are you doing here, girl?"

At that instant the dancer, eyes dilated with apprehension, also spoke: "What do you here, Nial?"

Conan answered with feigned carelessness: "The priests told me to fix a loose fitting on the offering chest."

"At this time of night? Which priest?" The girl's voice was sharp with tension.

Conan shrugged. "I don't remember."

"I do not believe you."

"And why not, pray?" said Conan with an air of offended innocence.

"Because such orders would have come only through me as Mistress of the Properties. You came here to steal. That is sacrilege."

"Now Rudabeh dear, you know what fakers and lechers these priests are—"

"But Zath is still a god, whatever the shortcomings of his—but Nial darling, whatever you came for, you must get you hence at once! The priests from Arenjun have just arrived. They were held up by a storm, which washed out the roads, and so missed the Festival of All Gods. Now Lord Feridun is showing them round the temple; they will soon be here. The new Vicar, Mirzes, sent me hither to see that the reservoir of the eternal flame was full, since we haven't had time to fill it lately."

To confirm her words, the sound of many men moving and talking outside the huge front doors of the naos smote Conan's ears.

"Go quickly!" cried Rudabeh, "or you will be lost!"

"I'm going," growled Conan. Instead of heading for a door, he gathered his tools and torch and ran to the far left corner of the sacred enclosure, where the oil pipe jutted out from the wall. Directly beneath it lay a large trapdoor.

As Conan stooped and shot back the bolt that held down the trapdoor, Rudabeh gave a cry of consternation. "What are you doing?"

"Going below," grunted Conan as he grasped the handle and raised the trapdoor. An overpowering stench of carrion wafted up out of the square black opening.

"Do not go there!" cried Rudabeh in anguished tones, her voice rising with terror. "You know not what you—oh, gods, here come the priests!"

The handles of the great bronze front doors clanked, and the doors themselves began to creak open, as a confabulation of voices reached the chamber from the vestibule. With a rush of feet and a slam of the side door, Rudabeh dashed out of the naos; Conan, glaring about like a hunted animal, bounded down the stair that descended from the temple floor into the reeking darkness below. He dropped the trap-door into place over his head, leaving himself in darkness save for the flickering orange light of the small torch.

The massive doors groaned open, and the swell of conver-sation rolled across the marble floor and through the thin planking of the trapdoor. Conan caught the deep, bell-like tones of High Priest Feridun, but he could not distinguish words through the babble. At least the murmur of conversa-tion, bland and unctuous, betrayed no excitement, which it surely would have if any of those entering had caught sight of Rudabeh or himself.

Cautiously, Conan felt his way down the stone stair, peer-ing ahead as far as the torch could throw its feeble beams. He found himself in a spacious passage, higher than his head and wider than his outstretched arms. No sound save the hiss of the flaring torch, so faint as to be barely audible even to his keen ears, dispelled the sepulchral silence. The smell of carrion rowelled his nostrils.

As Conan prowled along the rock-hewn floor of the pas-sage, he stumbled over a large object of irregular shape. It proved to be the skull of a bovine—or rather such a skull to which scraps of flesh still adhered. Conan kicked this noisome bit of carrion aside and plodded on, stepping over more fragments of kine—legs, ribs, and other parts. Although no stranger to the stink of corpses and cadavers, the soft squilch of a patch of rotting entrails, on which he stepped, so revolted him that for an instant he almost vom-ited, and fought down a panicky urge to run screaming.

Coming to a cross tunnel, Conan turned left and walked a few steps along that corridor, which sloped sharply up. He was, he reckoned, still beneath the temple. At the top of the slope, he thought, he would find the door on the west side, through which he had seen the flock of sheep driven.

He went back to the crossing and took the branch that ran straight from the steps down which he had come. This pas-sage, he found, sloped down. Conan continued for some moments, spurning desiccated animal fragments with his moccasins. When the tunnel turned this way and that and sent out branches, so that Conan feared getting lost in the maze, he retraced his steps to the first crossing.

Then he tried the remaining passage, which had been the right-hand branch when he first reached the intersection. The corridor ran straight for a bowshot, then wavered and sent out side passages as the downward-sloping tunnel had done.

Conan began to worry about his torch. It would not last much longer, and to be lost in this catacomb in utter darkness might prove fatal. He had a spare torch thrust through his belt under the apron; but, if he let the first torch die completely before lighting the second from it, he would have the devil's own time igniting the other with flint and steel in darkness. On the other hand, if he lit the second torch sooner than necessary, it, too, would be exhausted that much sooner.

Conan continued warily, thrusting the weak amber glow of the torch into openings in the sides of the tunnel and peering as far as the feeble light allowed his vision to range. He still came upon bones and other fragments of animals. Above the reek of carrion, another smell assailed his keen barbarian nostrils—the scent of a living creature, but one completely alien to him. The odor emanated from no beast or reptile that he knew of; nor yet from any plant or foodstuff with which he was familiar. The odor was unique—acrid but not altogether unpleasant.

As he moved stealthily, straining his eyes and ears, he thought he heard a faint repeated click, such as would be made by a horny object striking against the stone. He could not be sure that he heard aright, realizing that the horror of the tunnel had disoriented his senses and might be leading him to imagine things.

For one wild instant, he wondered whether the statue of Zath in the naos had, in fact, come to life and followed him down into the tunnels. Reason assured him that the onyx spider-god still squatted on its pedestal in the temple. If it had come to life while the High Priest was showing the place to his sacerdotal visitors, Conan would have heard some susurrant echo of the resulting hubub in the sanctum above.

Still, *something*—and of gigantic dimensions—had devoured the animals whose remains littered the floor of the tunnels. Suddenly Conan, who feared little on the earth that he trod, or in the seas, or in the ambient air above, found himself trembling at the implications of this thought.

He took a few steps down one of the side tunnels, holding high his torch, but saw nothing save some ghostly, whitened bones of a sheep or a goat. He worked his way back to the main corridor and tried another branch, with no happier result; for this branch soon came to a blind end.

He was certain, now, that the clicking sounds were not born of his febrile imagination. The cadenced crepitation seemed to be coming closer, although from which direction he could not tell. With a horror of being cornered at the end of the short branch tunnel, he hastened back to the main corridor.

For an instant Conan stood statuelike, his torch upraised and his head turning from side to side as he strove to locate the source of the sound. It came, he was now convinced, from further on in this branch of the tunnel, and rapidly waxed in volume.

His skin crawled with nameless terror as the clicks became louder, although he could not perceive their source. Then, just beyond the limit of his torchlight, something moved. As this object approached, Conan saw, reflected in the light of his torch, four spots of brightness in the tunnel at about breast level.

As the unwavering lights grew larger, they seemed to spread out and become four great jewels, such as might decorate the breastplate of an approaching warrior-king. But they were no such ornaments. Behind the four lights loomed an indeterminate bulk. Unable to distinguish details, Conan drew his blacksmith's hammer from its belt loop. Because of the need for silence, he had left his sword back in his quarters.

The lights seemed to halt at the periphery of his torch-light. The clicking stopped, then resumed; the lights drew closer, and behind them Conan caught a nightmarish impression of a vast hairy bulk propelled by many legs.

Conan whirled and ran, the wind of his motion causing his torch to flare up to a bright golden flame. Behind him came the relentless clicking of colossal claws on the stone, closer and ever closer.

Before he realized it, Conan had crossed the main intersection of the tunnels, the one he had first come upon after entering the subterranean system. Too late he decided that his best chance for escape would have been to go back to the trapdoor, burst out, and—if the priests were still in the naos—to confront them openly. The next best alternative would have been to turn to the right and take the downward-sloping tunnel, on the chance that it would issue into the outer world beyond the bounds of wall-girt Yezud.

He started to turn back. But it was too late for that; the four glowing eyes, reflecting the saffron light of the torch, had already reached the main crossing and blocked his way. He was trapped in this branch of the tunnel.

Conan continued his flight up the rising slope. At the top he came to a massive door, which he felt certain was the temple door through which the sheep had been admitted. Shaking with apprehension, he set down his hammer, fumbled for the Clavis of Gazrik, and applied it to the keyhole. When he uttered the spell, he heard the lock clank and pushed on the knob. But the door would not yield. Then Conan remembered that this door was also closed by a heavy bolt on the outside.

Remembering how he had used the silver arrow on his way into the temple, Conan aimed the arrow to the height where he supposed this bolt to be and repeated: *"Kapinin achilir genishi!"* more loudly. When nothing happened, he shouted the phrase with the full power of his huge lungs.

Instead of the sound of the bolt's motion, the next thing that Conan noticed was that the silver arrow was growing hot in his fingers. When it became too hot to hold he dropped it. As he did so it glowed, briefly, dull red; as it struck the floor, it softened and melted into an amorphous puddle, which quickly cooled and solidified. Then Conan remembered Parvez's words, that the Clavis of Gazrik would move a door bolt *if* it were not too heavy. He had evidently overtaxed the powers of the talisman and ruined it. It served him right, he thought, for using magic.

Conan pulled out his hammer and gave the door a furious blow. The portal boomed but remained immobile. Conan could see where he had dented the tough ironwood, without affecting the door's security. With such hard wood, it would take him an hour with hammer and chisel to force his way through the barrier.

He would have struck again, in a frenzy of desperation, but clickings behind him warned him to turn. As he did so, he found that the colossal spider—a living duplicate of the statue in the temple, save that this creature was covered with stiff hairs as long as a man's fingers—was upon him. Reflections of the flame of his torch danced in the four great round eyes across the creature's front.

Below these eyes, a pair of hairy, jointed appendages extended forward like arms. As these organs reached out for Conan, he smote one of them with his hammer, feeling the horny integument yield as it cracked. The spider recoiled a step, folding its injured limb beneath its hairy body.

Then the monster advanced again. It reared up on its six hindmost legs and spread the first pair, together with the uninjured palm, to seize its prey. Conan felt like a fly caught in a web, awaiting its fate.

Below the palps he could see the spider's fangs, a pair of curved, shiny, sharp-pointed organs like the horns of a bull, curving out and then inwards, so that the points almost met. They, too, now spread horizontally to pierce Conan's body from opposite sides; green venom dripped from their hollow points. Between and below the fangs, the jointed mouth parts worked hungrily.

For a heartbeat the pair confronted each other, Conan with his hammer raised to deliver one last crushing blow before he died, the spider with its monstrous, hairy appendages spread to grip the man in a last embrace.

From behind Zath, Conan heard Rudabeh's voice, raised in shrill tones of terror: "Nial! Dearest! I have—"

At this anguished cry, the spider backed away from Conan. It turned, so that one of its lateral eyes flashed briefly in the torchlight. Its great sack of an abdomen brushed against the wall of the narrow space, and Zath started toward the voice. Conan heard one frightful shriek; then silence, save for the diminishing click of horny claws on stone. At that instant, Conan's torch went out.

With a yell of fury, Conan started to run after the spider in total darkness, but he missed his direction and crashed into the wall of the tunnel. Getting shakily to his feet, he pulled the second torch from his belt. He cursed like a madman. The rag at the end of the first torch still glowed a dull red, like a lump of lava spat from a volcano.

Conan touched the ends together and blew frantic breaths until the second torch flared up. Dropping the exhausted torch, Conan ran down the ramp in pursuit of Zath.

At the main crossing, he slowed as his torch illumined something sprawled on the floor of the tunnel—something that was not the putrid remains of a cow or a sheep. Dreading what he knew he would find, he approached Rudabeh's body. She looked as if she slept; but when he knelt and pressed an ear to her breast, he could detect no heartbeat.

He leaned his torch against the tunnel wall to free both hands and examined her more closely. She wore the gauzy, fluttery garments that the dancing girls appeared in when they sang in chorus. He ripped away these obscuring filaments and turned over her finely-formed torso. On one shoulder and in the middle of her back he found a pair of puncture wounds, each surrounded by an area of blackened flesh where the injected spider's venom had taken effect.

He called: "Rudabeh! My love! Speak!" He chafed her hands and rhythmically pressed her ribs in hope of starting her breathing. Nothing had any effect.

Hot tears ran down Conan's rugged countenance—the first he had shed in many years. He angrily wiped them away, but still they flowed. Those who knew Conan as a man of iron, hard, merciless, and self-seeking, would have been astonished to see him weeping in that charnel house, heedless of his own safety.

The girl must, he thought, have braved these stinking tunnels, after the priests had gone, to warn him of his peril. To have another lay down life to save his was a unique event in Conan's experience, and the knowledge of her sacrifice filled him with pity, shame, and self-loathing.

Then rage surged like molten iron through his veins, and he picked up his torch and hammer, glaring about. The spider, he thought, must have dropped its burden when the light of Conan's torch alarmed it, and then retreated to that part of the tunnel where he first had met the brute.

With a yell of uncontrolled fury, Conan ran headlong down the tunnel branch where he had first encountered Zath, his torch flaring up with the fetid wind of his motion. He must have run a quarter of a league, shouting: "Zath! Show yourself and fight!" But no sign of the giant arachnid did he see.

Breathing heavily, he gave up the chase. If Zath were in this branch of the tunnel, he would surely have by now overtaken it in its lumbering flight. Perhaps it was hiding in one of the many cross passages and side chambers, but to explore them all would require days.

He retraced his steps until he found himself back at the main crossing. Now cold to the touch, Rudabeh lay where he had left her. He would not abandon her in this stinking hellhole for Zath to consume, because he had a barbarian's superstitious fear of failing to bury the body of one of his kith and kin.

Such a person's ghost, he had learned as a boy, would haunt him in revenge for his neglect. Since he had few friends and no kinsmen in civilized lands, he had not felt compelled to bury any of the many corpses that he had seen in late years. Besides, Rudabeh had been the one human being whom he had truly loved and who had loved him in return since he had left his bleak homeland, and he would not desert her now. He would somehow get her out of the tunnels to some lonely place, where he would dig a grave, with his bare hands if need be, and lay her in it. He would pile rocks on the grave against wolves and hyenas, place a single wildflower atop the stones, and go his way.

He picked up the girl's body, slung it over one massive shoulder, and started back along the tunnel that led to the trapdoor. Surely, he thought, the priests would have retired by this late hour, leaving the naos deserted. At the end of the corridor he set down the cold corpse, climbed the steps, and listened against the underside of the trapdoor.

To his surprise, the sound of voices filtered through to him. He made out the deep tones of the High Priest, the higher ones of Mirzes, and a third voice he did not know. Feridun's leonine roar came through to him:

"Zath curse your eyeballs, Darius! You promised us fair weather for the three days of the festival; instead of which, you allowed our guests to depart in a downpour! Where is the skill at commanding the spirits of the air whereof you have boasted? If you cannot do better than that, we shall have to give the task of weather magic to another."

Darius mumbled something apologetic, but then Mirzes the new Vicar spoke: "I suspect, Holiness, that Darius did it a-purpose, to diminish your repute and thus further his own political designs."

"Naught of the sort!" protested Darius. "I have never. . . ." Then all three spoke at once, so that Conan could no longer distinguish words.

Conan thought of bursting into the naos, laying Rudabeh's body on the offering chest, chiseling out the Eyes of Zath, and fleeing. This was obviously impractical while the chamber was occupied. A wild idea crossed his mind, of pushing up the trapdoor and confronting the priests with the body. But Conan had no sword, and the priests had only to shout to bring the Brythunian guards on the run.

He quickly abandoned this suicidal idea. If the priests discovered, as they surely would, that Rudabeh had been in collusion with Conan, they might not bury her properly, either. Nor could he pry out the Eyes with one hand while fighting off Catigern's mercenaries with the other. There was nothing for it but to manage the burial himself and come back later for the jewels, when the naos was vacant.

With a heavy sigh he descended, picked up the body, and set forth. At the main crossing he continued straight on, down the slope of the central passage. Where the tunnel branched, he followed what seemed to be the main corridor.

XII.   The Children of Zath

Suddenly, the tunnel opened out into a vast cavern, where stalactites hung from the roof over stalagmites that reared up from the floor to meet them. Directly before Conan, half a dozen stone steps led down to the floor of the cavern, so that he had a clear view across to the further wall. The feeble light of his torch could not throw its amber beams so far; but in the midst of the distant blackness appeared an opening to the outer world. Through this aperture Conan sighted a patch of night sky, in which a star glimmered. Evidently the rain clouds of the previous day had rolled away.

Within the cave entrance, below the actual aperture, was another patch of dim luminescence. Conan's keen vision identified this as a circular pool of water, reflecting the night sky outside and blocking the entrance to the cave. The strange odor which he had sensed before his encounter with Zath assailed his nostrils with nauseating intensity.

All about the floor of the cave, the flickering orange light showed large, lumpish things scattered here and there among the stalagmites, like giant mushrooms of mottled gray-and-brown coloring. As Conan began to descend the steps, intending to pick his way among these obstacles to the exit, motion caught his eye. When he looked more closely, he saw that one of the supposed fungi was coming to life. It unfolded jointed legs, raised its body from the ground, and turned four gleaming eyes on Conan.

The thing was a duplicate, in miniature, of Zath, although its dimensions were only half those of the original spider-god. Still, it was larger than the giant spider that Conan had fought in the Tower of the Elephant years before. One such monster could easily kill Conan, and there must be hundreds in the cavern.

The first spider to awaken started toward Conan, while on all sides other giant spiders were coming to life and rising to their clawed feet. Within a few heartbeats of Conan's first appearance in the cave, the monster arachnids were streaming toward him. The click of their claws on the stone rose to a continuous rattle. Wherever Conan looked, quartets of gleaming eyes caught the light of his torch.

Conan whirled and ran back up the long slope of the tunnel, while his hearing told him that the entire swarm was crowding into the tunnel behind him and racing after him, like a jointed-legged flood. On, on he went. At first, to judge from the diminishing sounds behind him, he gained on his pursuers. But, heavily burdened, he was forced to slow down, while his heart labored and his breath came in gasps. Then the castanetlike sound of hundreds of horny claws on the stone came closer. These, he realized, must be the Children of Zath of whom the High Priest had spoken.

Ever the rough walls of the tunnel fled past. Without the body, Conan was sure he could outrun the spiders; but it inevitably slowed him down. Still, he would not abandon it. He had the feeling of being in a nightmare, where one runs and runs through darkness while an unseen menace comes ever closer behind. He feared that he must have taken a wrong fork and would be lost forever in this maze.

When he was almost in despair, he found himself at the main crossing. He kept straight on and soon reached the stair to the trapdoor.

At the end of the tunnel, Conan climbed the steps and listened. He heard no sound from above—no talking, shuffling, or other indication of human activity. Perhaps the accursed priests had gone to bed at last. In these hours between midnight and morning, all in the temple, save the Brythunian guards on night duty, should be sound asleep. Conan did not know how he could escape unnoticed from the temple with Rudabeh's body; but, with the clatter of claws of

the Children of Zath coming closer, he had no time to concoct a clever scheme.

With the fist that held the torch, he pushed against the
trapdoor. The square of planking failed to move. With a
silent curse, Conan wondered if someone had noticed that
the bolt had been shot back and replaced it.

With the crepitation of the Children's claws coming
closer, Conan was not about to let a mere bolt stop him now.
If a good push would not dislodge it, he could break through
the trap with his hammer, although he would have preferred
not to do so because of the noise.

He stepped back down to the tunnel floor and set down
Rudabeh's body. Then he leaned his torch against the tunnel
wall. Again he mounted the steps, put both hands against
the underside of the trap, and gave a terrific heave.

The trap rose against resistance, as if someone had placed
a heavy weight upon it. Then suddenly the resistance ceased;
there was a sharp cry, the thump of a falling body, and the
trap flew open.

As Conan leaped out into the gloom, a stream of oil struck
him and cascaded over his clothing. By the wavering light of
the eternal flame in its bowl, he saw a priest, whom he recognized as Mirzes, the Vicar, sprawled on the floor and
beginning to rise. Beside him lay a large pitcher on its side,
and a pool of oil spread out from it across the marble.

In a flash, Conan understood. When Rudabeh had disappeared instead of reporting back to the Vicar, Mirzes had
doubtless searched for her. Failing to find her, he had under-
taken the task of refilling the reservoir himself. He had been
standing on the trapdoor and directing the stream of bitumen into his pitcher when Conan's sudden emergence had
thrown him off the planking.

Mirzes started to scramble up, crying: "Who—what—
Nial! What in the seven hells—" But then his feet slipped on
the oily surface, and he fell again.

Conan leaped out on the floor and turned toward Mirzes,
but his feet skidded also. He staggered and recovered.

"Help!" croaked Mirzes. "Guards!"

Slipping and scrambling, Conan reached Mirzes just as
the priest regained his feet. As Mirzes opened his mouth to
cry another alarm, Conan whipped his fist up against the

Vicar's chin with a meaty smack, hurling the slight priest back on the mosaic floor unconscious.

Standing over his victim, Conan thought of finishing him off with a skull-cracking blow of his hammer. But with the hammer in his hand, he drew back from his bloodthirsty resolution. To slay a man while that man was asleep or otherwise helpless went against his notions of honor. He thought of cutting Mirzes' turban into lengths to bind and gag the priest.

But it was more urgent to recover his torch and Rudabeh's body and to bolt the trapdoor, before the Children of Zath swarmed up into the naos. Conan started back toward the recess in the wall, aware that the faucet had remained open and that the abundant stream of bitumen continued to pour down into the tunnel. He must quickly turn off the valve; once the flow was stopped and the trap securely bolted, he could turn his attention back to Mirzes.

After that, Conan thought, he would try to pry out the Eyes from the spider idol. To escape from the temple, he would pound on the front door and shout for help. When the Brythunians unlocked and opened the doors, Conan would cry "Murder! Robbery! Help the Vicar!" When the guards rushed in, he would slip past them and out.

Conan had taken but two steps toward the trapdoor when, with a thunderous belching sound, a mass of flame and smoke erupted out of the square opening in the floor. The oil had come in contact with Conan's torch in the tunnel. Conan made one desperate effort to reach the faucet, but the flames drove him back with singed hair and eyebrows, frantically beating out a small fire started in his oil-soaked clothing.

Realizing at last that he could do nothing more for Rudabeh's body, he sprang to the statue and began fumbling for tools, to extract at least one Eye before the conflagration drove him forth. Smoke rolled out, thicker and thicker, until it set Conan to coughing and prevented him from even seeing clearly enough to work on the jewels in the statue.

Stubbornly, he continued to try to place a drill in the proper position. He got in one stroke of his hammer and was pleased to see the point of the drill bite into the lead. But the smoke so afflicted him with coughing that he could only clutch at the nearest stone spider leg, gasping and retching.

Then the light in the naos brightened, and through the billowing smoke Conan saw that a wall hanging was going up in flame. From outside the naos he heard cries of "Fire! Fire!"

The smoke momentarily lifted; and Conan, glancing toward the flaming recess with the trapdoor, saw a sight that wrung a shudder from him. A colossal gray-and-brown spider was hoisting itself out of the trapdoor. Its massive bulk scraped against the sides of the opening as it forced its hairy body through the aperture, like some demon rising from a flaming hell. Zath had escaped its tunnel-prison at last.

Out it came, swiveling about on its jointed legs, and sighted Conan. As the scuttling horror started for its prey, the Cimmerian ran for the front door, putting away his tools as he went. He seized the bronzen door handles and tried to thrust open the doors, but they were still locked. A glance behind showed that the spider was close upon him.

Then a key clicked in the lock and the doors opened. Conan found himself facing the startled countenances of two Brythunians, one of whom held a large key. Others crowded behind the mercenaries. Smoke had already seeped out the cracks around these doors, alerting the people of the temple.

Conan staggered, coughing, out of the naos and into a scene of wild confusion. Priests of Zath, visiting priests from Arenjun, acolytes, dancing girls, mercenaries, and slaves ran in all directions. Priests bawled commands.

Through the smoke loomed Zath in the doorway. At the sight, everyone in the vestibule broke into mad flight for the nearest exit. The small door in the outer valves was jammed with several fugitives trying to get through it at once.

Forcing his way to the door by sheer strength, Conan seized the handles of the main door, wrenched them around, and pushed the groaning valves open. Those clustered against the door boiled out, falling, tripping over one another, and scrambling up to run. Conan glimpsed a pair of acolytes hustling the former Vicar out of the temple, while Harpagus stared about in childlike wonder.

Conan bounded down the front steps two at a time. Halfway down he turned to snatch a look back. Thick smoke poured out of the open portal. Overhead the night was clear and star-dusted, while a half moon stood high in the eastern sky.

In the open front portal stood two figures. One was the giant spider; its long hairs had been mostly singed off, but it seemed otherwise uninjured. The other, almost within arm's length of the monster, was the lean, hawk-nosed figure of High Priest Feridun, in his white robe and black turban. The priest was making passes with his hands and chanting some rigmarole.

With its forelegs raised as if to seize Feridun, Zath paused. The priest continued his incantation, raising his voice to a shout and frantically gesturing, so that his long white beard lashed the smoky night air. The two grotesque figures were silhouetted against the lurid glare of the fire behind them. The spider retreated a step, back toward the naos; then another step. The priest's fabled control over animals could even force this monster to immolate itself in the blaze.

Then Feridun got a lungful of smoke and went into a spell of coughing. Instantly, the spider, no longer constrained by its master's voice, darted forward. Its great jointed limbs enfolded the priest, who screamed once.

A burly figure in mail dashed past Conan up the steps, waving a sword. From the flowing red hair Conan recognized Captain Catigern. Reaching the top, the Brythunian took a cut at the spider's body, opening a gash from which a dark fluid seeped. Zath, who had issued from the portal and now stood on the topmost step, dropped the priest's body and turned upon its new adversary. As it spread its appendages, Catigern backed away, swinging his sword right and left. The spider followed, keeping just beyond reach of the blade.

"Hold on, Catigern!" shouted Conan between coughs. He had sighted, lying on the steps, a halberd belonging to one of the guards on duty at the main entrance. The Brythunian had dropped it when he fled.

Pounding up the steps, Conan snatched up the polearm. Coming up on the side of Zath, he swung the halberd high over his head and, with every ounce of power that he possessed, brought it whistling down on the forward segment of the monster.

The axe blade sank deeply into the spider's leathery flesh, and such was the force of the stroke that the shaft broke off midway from butt to head. Ponderously, Zath turned toward Conan. Running in from the other side, Catigern drove his sword in deeply above the base of the second leg and wrenched it out.

Zath began to turn back toward the Brythunian, but it moved more and more slowly. Before it completed its turn, its legs gave way, dropping its body to the marble steps, which became fouled with the dark ichor that dripped from its wounds. Its sprawling legs continued to twitch, but these movements slowly dwindled. Zath was dead.

Catigern seized Conan around the shoulders in a fierce hug. "Thank all the gods you came along! Any time you want a lieutenancy in my company, do but ask."

"I'll think about it," said Conan, coughing.

Another Brythunian approached. "Captain, the priest Dinak wants our help in fighting the fire."

Seeing the spider dead, Yezudites began crowding back into the square before the temple. The citizens boiled out of their houses, some in nightwear and some in hastily donned work garments. The priests dashed about organizing fire fighting. Thick, oily smoke continued to roll out the doors of the temple.

"Bear a hand!" shouted Catigern in Conan's ear, shoving a bucket into his grip. "Get into yonder line!"

Conan had been about to turn away and go to the smithy, collect his gear, and shake the dust of Yezud from his feet. The temple of Zath was an evil fane, even more obnoxious than most Zamorian cults. He cared nothing for its architectural splendor, and if more priests were destroyed in the conflagration, that was all right with him. If he could not bury Rudabeh, to burn the temple for her funeral pyre was the next best thing. With her gone, there was no one in Yezud for whose fate Conan cared.

Well, that was not quite true. Captain Catigern had become a friend, and each had saved the other's life. If the Brythunian were locked in battle with the fire, it behooved Conan to give him a hand.

The sky had begun to pale with the approach of dawn; but then it suddenly clouded over. A small but very black cloud formed over Yezud. A flash of lightning paled the flames licking out around the base of the central dome, and a roll of thunder drowned out the roar of the flames. Down came rain, but such rain as Conan had never seen. It was like standing under a waterfall.

Conan took his place in the bucket line and, with rain running down his face, handed buckets back and forth in a steady rhythm. The buckets were filled at the fountain in the temple square and were passed back to Yezudites around and within the fane.

With a roaring crash, the central dome collapsed and disappeared. A cloud of sparks, smoke, and dust billowed up from the gap; rain poured into it. Little by little, between the fire fighters and the rain, the fire was beaten back; it had been confined to the naos.

The Yezudites were still battling the flames, and the sun, though not yet visible, was tinging the scattered dawn clouds crimson when Conan slipped away from the temple. Soon after, somewhat cleaned up and booted, he appeared at the stable with his saddle over one shoulder and a blanket roll over the other. The groom on duty, a stolid youth named Yazdan, looked up as the Cimmerian pushed into the stalls. He asked:

"What would you, Master Nial? I thought you had lost your steed!"

"One of them," grunted Conan, striding down the row of stalls to that housing Egil. "This one's mine, also."

"Ho? What say you?" cried Yazdan. "You must be mad! That unmanageable beast belongs to the temple; Vicar Harpagus brought him back from his travels."

"After he stole him from me!" roared Conan. "Stand aside, boy, if you don't wish to be hurt!"

"I cannot—Zath's curse would—" protested the youth, striving to block Conan's advance with outstretched arms.

"I'm sorry to do this," grated Conan, dropping his burdens. "But you give me no choice."

He picked up Yazdan, who kicked and flailed the air, and slammed the groom against the wall. Yazdan sagged to the floor, half unconscious. Minutes later, Conan led a saddled Egil out of the stable; the horse whinnied and took little dancing steps with the pleasure of being reunited with his old master.

Conan stopped at Bartakes's Inn to buy extra provisions—a loaf, a slab of meat, and a leather bottle of ale—for his journey. He was counting out coins to a yawning Bartakes, whom he had routed out of bed, when a familiar voice said:

"Aha, there you are! I wondered what had become of you." Captain Catigern, still filthy with soot and ash, had his arm in a sling. He continued: "From the blanket roll on your horse, I'd say you were planning to leave us."

"I might," said Conan, "if I had a better prospect elsewhere. What befell your arm?"

"A beam fell on me, and I think the bone is cracked. I'll get a chirurgeon as soon as may be. When I saw the fire was under control, I turned command over to Gwotelin."

"How much of the temple burned?"

"The naos is an indescribable mess; the falling roof timbers smashed that damned spider idol into a hundred pieces. But elsewhere the damage was only slight; most of the building is stone, and the oil stopped flowing out that pipe in the naos. I suppose the pool that feeds it ran dry."

"Will this end the cult of Zath?"

"Mitra, no! They are already talking of rebuilding. I'll wager they'll choose Darius their new high priest, for that his rain spell saved most of the building. There should be plenty of work for a craftsman like you."

"No doubt, but I have other plans." Conan thought, the Eyes of Zath, if not smashed to fragments by the fall of the dome, would have been baked by the heat to plain white stones of no value. At least, he thought with vindictive relish, if he could not enjoy them, neither could anyone else.

"That is your business," said Catigern. "By the bye, that black stallion looks uncommonly like one of the temple's horses."

"Egil is mine," growled Conan. "Some day I'll tell you how Harpagus stole him from me. If you doubt me, I'll show you how he answers to my voice."

"I am in no condition to gainsay you," said Catigern. "At least, with a new High Priest, let us hope there will be no more giant spiders."

"Whence did Feridun get that one?"

Catigern shrugged, then winced at the sudden pain in his injured arm. "I know not. Perchance it was a leftover from some bygone era; or perchance he grew it by sorcery from an ordinary tarantula."

"What's become of the last two Vicars?"

"Harpagus is still out of his mind, and Mirzes is dead. We found him in the naos, apparently suffocated by smoke."

"Good!" growled Conan.

Catigern looked keenly at the Cimmerian. "That reminds me. One of my men swears he saw you come rushing out of the naos with the spider hot behind you, although no one had seen you go in. Might there be a connection betwixt your unauthorized visit and the death of Mirzes?"

"There might," said Conan. "But there is something else you should know." He described the cavern with the swarming Children of Zath. "The spider must have laid a clutch of eggs after Feridun installed her in the tunnels. If the King didn't give in, Feridun would unleash the horde on Zamora. I think there must be some means of draining that pool, to let the Children escape their cave and scatter over the countryside."

Catigern whistled. "Then the real spider was a female, for all that they call Zath a male god! And these creatures are still there?"

"Unless the river of flaming oil, running down into the cavern, has cooked them. I suppose it did, or they'd have swarmed up out of their burrow as did the big one."

"This I must see," mused the Brythunian. "Can you show me the cave entrance?"

Conan shook his head. "It is somewhere in these hills; but you could search for a month without finding it. You'd better go down through the trapdoor, as I did."

Catigern shuddered. "I must lead my men into that hole with pikes and torches, to make sure all those vermin are dead," he muttered. "Feridun was honest in his way, but the gods preserve me from fanatics!"

"I'm told he controlled beasts of all kinds," said Conan, yawning prodigiously. "If he'd lost his spiders but survived, he might have set wolves or lions or eagles on the Zamorians. Well, I must away."

Catigern accompanied Conan out the door, musing: "There are mysteries here, which the priests will want me to investigate. I shall be glad not to pry into the doings of one who has twice saved my hide, not to mention thwarting the High Priest's mad plan."

Conan wrung the hand of the Catigern's uninjured arm and began to unhitch his horse when he spied the barrel of bitumen, for Bartakes's lamps, standing around the corner of the inn.

Conan left the horse and opened the door. "Mandana!" he called.

"Aye?" The innkeeper's daughter came out of the kitchen, wiping her hands on her apron.

Conan turned to Catigern. "Farewell, friend. I would have a word with the damsel alone."

Catigern grinned wolfishly and entered the tavern. Conan said: "Mandana, will you step out here? I have somewhat to say."

Misinterpreting Conan's grim smile, the girl came forward with alacrity, simpering. "So, have you tired of that skinny temple wench at last?"

"I shall never see her again," said Conan. "Ere he went mad, Harpagus the Vicar told me that you had informed him of Rudabeh's visit to the inn."

"What if I did? She deserved it for violating her temple's rules and coming down here to lure away my patrons. How are we to live, with such unfair competition?"

Conan nodded sagely. "I'll show you something." He stepped to the barrel and threw off the lid. "Now," he said, clutching Mandana about the waist and swinging her off her feet.

"Nial!" she cried. "Not here in the mud! You barbarians are so impetuous! I have a fine bed upstairs—"

"Aye," grunted Conan. With a stride he towered over the barrel. Bending over, with the laughing girl still clutched about the waist, he dipped her flowing black mane into the tarlike fluid.

So speedy and so accurate was his move that Mandana did not suspect his true intention until her scalp was immersed in the black, sticky oil. Then she screamed.

In a single, sweeping motion, Conan raised and set her on her feet. She stood for a moment transfixed, with tar running down her plump, pink cheeks to drip on her bodice. Frantically, she ran her hands through the ropelike strands of hair, stared at the viscous substance that befouled them, and shrieked wordlessly.

"Your just desert for tattling," rumbled Conan. "By the time your shaven skull has grown a new crop, perhaps you'll have learned to mind your own affairs."

Conan unhitched his horse and swung into the saddle. Pursued by screams of "I hate you! I hate you!" he trotted briskly away on the Shadizar road.

Where the narrow valley below Yezud opened out, Conan rode past Kharshoi and into the more spacious lands of central Zamora. The sun being well past its zenith, Conan drew rein on a rise in the road, whence he had a good view of the route by which he had come. Yawning, he pulled a fowl's leg and a biscuit out of his saddle bag and sat cross-legged on the ground, eating, while Egil, reins trailing, cropped the grass behind him. Sleep plucked seductively at Conan's elbow, for he had had none the night before; but he dared not relax until he was farther from Yezud.

Suddenly there came a disturbance in the air before Conan, as if a tiny dust-devil had formed. The dust cleared, and there stood Psamitek the Stygian, holding a small brass tripod with a little smoking brazier at its apex. While Conan gaped with astonishment, the Stygian stooped and set the tripod on the ground. He made passes over it, chanting in some guttural tongue that Conan did not know.

"What the devil?" cried Conan, scrambling to his feet and reaching for his scimitar. "By Crom, this time—"

As he spoke, Psamitek shouted a word. Thereupon the sapphire smoke from the tripod instantly compacted itself into a ropelike column, writhing like a pale-blue, translucent serpent in the still afternoon air.

Another gesture and word from the Stygian, and the blue serpentine of smoke whipped toward Conan like a striking snake. The smoky cord threw coils around Conan's body, like some ghostly python, pinioning his sword arm with his scimitar half drawn. Another coil wrapped itself around

Conan's neck and tightened, cutting off the Cimmerian's breath.

Conan struggled until he foamed at the mouth. With his free left hand he clawed at the loop of smoke around his throat, so that his tunic bulged with the desperate bunching of muscles beneath it. To his touch the smoke felt like a cable of some slick, yielding, but animate substance, like a live eel, but dry.

He forced his thumb between the noose and his neck, although he had to gouge his own flesh with his thumbnail. He pulled the loop far enough from his throat to allow a wheezy, strangulated breath, but he might as well have tugged at a steel cable. The loop tightened, and Conan's face purpled. The veins in his temples swelled until they seemed likely to burst.

Psamitek smiled thinly. "I said you should see more of my little tricks. Now I shall at leisure collect your head and the reward therefor. I need not even divide it with that Turanian savage. I shall have the finest occult library in Stygia!"

Conan tried to bite into the noose but could not pull it far enough from his chin to get his teeth into it. He thought of trying to throw his dagger, but one of the loops of smoke had pinioned the weapon against his side. Behind him he heard Egil moving uneasily, watching the drama with anxious incomprehension.

At the spectacle of Conan's violent but unavailing struggles, Psamitek gave a coldly cynical laugh. "This," he purred, "gives me more pleasure than even the gladiatorial games of Argos!"

Before Conan's eyes, the landscape swam and darkened. With a final effort, he pulled the noose far enough from his throat to emit one shout. "Egil!" he croaked. "Kill him!"

With a snort, the well-trained war horse sprang past Conan and reared up at Psamitek. Conan had a glimpse of the Stygian's sallow countenance, suddenly wide-eyed with alarm at this unexpected intervention. And then one of Egil's hooves descended on Psamitek's shaven head with a crunch of shattered cranium.

Instantly the magical rope faded away, dissolving into wisps of ordinary smoke. Freed, Conan sank down, gasping great lungfuls of air.

When he had recovered, Conan heaved himself erect and tottered over to where Psamitek lay. He went through the Stygian's purse, finding an assortment of coins, some of them gold, and the roll of parchment bearing Tughril's offer for Conan's head. The money Conan transferred to his own purse.

The scroll he stared at, trying to puzzle out its spidery glyphs. It would not do, he thought, to leave such a document adrift in the world. Someone else might get his hands on it and be inspired, like Psamitek, to try to collect the reward.

Conan bent and gently blew upon the tiny, smoldering fire in the brazier; the little tripod still stood upright. When he had coaxed a flame into being, he dipped a corner of the parchment into the blaze and held it there until the writing surf... ...ght fire. He held the sheet, turning it to spread ... ...e across it. The cryptic writings glowed red for an instant and disappeared. Soon the entire document, save the corner by which Conan held it, was reduced to ash.

Then Conan swung into the saddle and cantered off, leaving the Stygian's body for the hyenas.

About the Author

L. SPRAGUE DE CAMP is well known for his
science popularizations and historical novels as well as
work in the science fiction world. His work appeared
many of the science fiction magazines of the 1930s, includ-
ing *Astounding* and *The Magazine of Fantasy and Science
Fiction*. De Camp has also worked on unfinished manuscripts of Robert E. Howard and, with Lin Carter, created
new Conan stories. He is the author of *The Science Fiction
Handbook*, a guide for writers on how to plot, write and sell
science fiction.